Letters Lost

Tina Sausa

SERENITY BOOKS

Printed in the United States of America.

ISBN# 13-978-099058159
ISBN# 10:0990581594
Library of Congress-in-publication Data

 Serenity Books Publishing

www.serenitybookpublishing.com

Tina Sausa

TABLE OF CONTENTS

Prologue 5

Miabella Maxima's Dilemma 9

Miabella's Mistake? 32

Miabella's Future 51

Rich Marvice's Nightmares 57

Laura Spelling's Plea 63

The Spellings' Fate 76

Marvice's Recurrent Dreams 95

Jonathan Wright's Attempt 98

Jonathan's Reconciliation 113

Marvice's Confession 120

Over the Next Ten Years 129

Prologue

ich Marvice could never imagine how his failure to deliver three letters would affect the lives of their senders—Miabella Maxima, Laura Spelling, and Jonathan Wright—and their intended recipients. He also didn't expect the personal turmoil he'd experience when various scenarios plagued his dreams during long, sleepless nights. Rich's troubles began on a rainy September day.

After close to one year of unemployment, Rich landed a job as a postal service carrier in the town of Caldwell, New Jersey, a peaceful, safe suburban area only twenty minutes from his home. After losing his previous job in October, he had been working various part-time jobs to support his wife Aggie and newborn son Jack. It didn't bother Rich that on this September morning, he'd be delivering mail during an intense, windy rainstorm. He kissed Aggie and Jack goodbye and headed out for his first day on his newfound job.

Walking along Main Street with a full mail pouch proved more challenging than Rich envisioned. He watched an elderly woman, whose bright yellow umbrella turned inside out as she fought to reshape it. A mother rushed her daughter into a storefront to get out of the rain, as the wind whipped against the buildings and the downpour soaked them. Nevertheless, Rich decided to make the best of this day because he truly appreciated being employed in such rough economic times.

With a positive, happy stride, Rich approached the mailbox located in front of the town civic center. He turned his key, opened the box, and removed the correspondence people placed in his care. He transferred almost all of the letters into his pouch when a strong gust of wind almost knocked him off his feet. *Wow, what a powerful one!* Rich steadied himself while trying to catch hold of the letters when he noticed three had escaped his grasp and were headed toward the sewer opening next to the street curb. He dashed through the wind gust like a boxer approaching a formidable opponent. Rich bent down and reached for the letters, but before he could snatch them, another blast of wind knocked him to his knees. All three letters swam into the sewer along a stream of water and disappeared from his sight.

Rich's upbeat mood sank into the sewer with the letters. *What now! How can I report losing mail to my supervisor my first day on the job?* Rich considered the security his paycheck would bring to his struggling family, and he knew he had only one choice—to forget he ever saw those letters. He'd always been a person of integrity with a conscience of a saint, yet he decided to keep the mishap from everyone, including his wife.

Chapter One

Miabella Maxima's Dilemma

"I'm totally in love with Alex!" Miabella Maxima declared to Vicky. Vicky Smith smiled, having heard these words from her BFF before.

"No, I mean it," Miabella added, seeing the look of disbelief on Vicky's face. "This time it's different. I know he loves me too. I can tell by the way he looks at me with those big, brown, puppy dog eyes, especially before he kisses me."

"And . . . tell me more," Vicky pleaded. Vicky lived vicariously through the more popular, well-endowed, prettier girl. She'd grown accustomed to Miabella getting all of the attention from the guys. In fact, when a boy met Vicky, he'd express interest in her friend. But Miabella didn't realize the effect she had on guys. Happy-go-lucky, kind, and not the least bit conceited, she also trusted everyone—a quality that Vicky worried about because she feared her friend could easily be hurt when it came to love.

Despite all of the attention, Miabella couldn't make a strong love connection with any of the guys who pursued her. Her "moral compass" directed her to live with high standards, especially when it came to sex—standards most young girls in 2014 could never follow. Fortunately, Alex hadn't pressured her about sex. He understood that she needed to take things slowly. But one year had passed since they first started going out, and she knew their relationship couldn't continue forever without her taking the next step.

"Well," Miabella said, with a shy sort of wickedness. "I can't help how I feel when I'm with Alex." Miabella crossed her arms in front of her and looked down at the plush cream-colored carpet.

"What do you mean?" Mia's body language confused Vicky.

"I have to stop myself from going further with him." Mia's face turned a few shades deeper, flushed with embarrassment and excitement.

Vicky squirmed in the pink plaid chair she often sits in whenever she's in Miabella's bedroom. "You're not saying you might sleep with him?" Vicky shrieked. Vicky knew it would take a mountain to fall before her friend would consider going all the way, even with a handsome athlete like Alex, who could have any girl he wanted.

"No! That's not what I'm saying," Miabella said, defending her honor. Apparently, Vicky didn't know her well enough. "I just said that I have to stop myself because I love him so much, and I feel great when I'm with him. It's hard for me."

"Okay," Vicky said, breathing a sigh of relief. She worried about Miabella getting carried away by Alex's persuasive demeanor and letting her guard down. Like Miabella said in the past, once you reach the point of no return, your compass crashes, and you can easily lose your way. Their friends would laugh hysterically as Miabella often referred to herself as the "only moral compass" in the group. Amazingly, none of the girls made fun of Miabella for her prudish ways—unless they only pretended to admire her.

Miabella remembered the day she fell for Alex Vasserman. They met in front of the student center building at William Paterson University on the first day of classes. The spring-like weather on this early September day brought back memories of the fleeting summer. Miabella sat perched on a large rock with Greek-letter graphite all over it, while she basked in the mild sun, her natural brunette curls revealing auburn highlights. She leaned back on the palms of her hands, with her chin toward the warm sun to tan her smooth-as-silk face and her hair sprawled loosely over the back of her petite-framed shoulders.

Miabella looked especially enticing to Alex—with her tight-fitting, ankle-length jeans and pink-and-red cropped top that revealed a firm midriff. Thoughts raced through his mind quicker than the beat of his pounding heart. As he wiped his sweaty palms on his T-shirt, he couldn't resist the urge to sit on the rock next to her and strike up a conversation. "You a freshman?" he asked.

"Why? Do I look like one?" she responded, as she opened her eyes to the model-like guy with the sexy, deep voice.

Alex let out a hearty laugh. "Not really, but I'm sure I would have noticed a girl as pretty as you on campus."

Miabella's face turned redder in one minute of Alex's presence than the thirty minutes she had spent applying makeup to get the same look. "Thanks for the compliment," she said, trying hard not to stare at this incredible-looking guy with the olive-like eyes, soft-looking light-brown hair, and a physique that would probably turn any woman's head. Alex wore a slightly weathered, pale-blue T-shirt, which hugged his body. Each muscle on his arms and chest stood out like delectable, bubbly cheese on the top of a pizza. His jeans were tight in all the right spots, and his sneakers were as clean as the new ones Miabella's mom bought her at the beginning of each school year. It didn't escape Miabella that several girls looked over at Alex as they passed by. Miabella couldn't resist gazing at him. "I guess you're not a freshman?"

"No, I'm a sophomore."

"How do you like WP?"

"It's good. The best part for me is baseball."

"You look like a baseball player," she said, before she could stop herself. *Oh, great! It sounds like I'm checking him out.*

"Yeah, girls say that," he admitted. A guilty-looking grin took over his tan face. *I think she's into me.*

Mia changed the subject. "What position do you play?"

"This year, I'll be one of the starting pitchers. I pitched a few games my freshman year, and the coaches were impressed."

"MAYBE, I'll come to one of your practices."

"Sure." *I wouldn't mind that.*

Mia didn't want the conversation to end. "What's your major?"

"Bio."

"I didn't declare my major yet, but I'm leaning toward biology too."

"I bet you're smart," Alex said.

Miabella avoided answering because she didn't want to brag. She received WP's top academic scholarship. "Do I look smart?" she asked.

Alex moved closer to Mia and gazed into her beautiful, dark green eyes. They shimmered in the sunlight like emeralds. "Let me have a look," he teased.

"OMG," Miabella said, rolling her eyes. "You're something else. By the way, why did you choose bio as a major?"

"Why do think? The female anatomy fascinates me." Miabella cracked a smile and turned away. Alex took a pencil from his back pocket and opened his notebook. "Can I have your number?" he asked, raising his eyebrows and widening his eyes. "What's your name?"

"It's Miabella," she answered. Mia twisted her sandal into a crack in the concrete. "What's yours?"

"Alex," he responded. "I'll call you soon."

After they exchanged phone numbers, Miabella rushed off to her next class. She didn't want to be late. Alex assumed the position Miabella had been in, basking in the sun as passerby admirers whispered comments to each other. Unlike Miabella, who didn't notice all of the guys who checked her out, Alex realized the effect he had on women. Whenever a pretty girl stared at him or said hi, he turned on his coaxing, effervescent smile, as though each girl appeared extra special to him. He loved every minute of the attention he received.

Miabella reflected on that special first day of her freshman year at WP when she met the most handsome guy in the world who sent shivers up her spine and continued to excite her every time they kissed. By the end of the first week of school, Alex asked Miabella to be his steady girlfriend. Overjoyed, she said yes. Miabella glowed with excitement as she reminisced about that day, giving details to Vicky.

"Vic, I think about him all the time. I daydream in class, and I struggle to keep focused on the teacher's lecture," Miabella said. "It's as though Alex is in the room with me, holding me." Miabella wrapped her hands around her shoulders, running them up and down her arms ever so slightly. She knew Vicky got a kick out of her dramatic style. Vicky rolled her eyes.

Miabella continued babbling, "Things are getting hot when we're together, Vic. That's why I'm having such a hard time. I don't know how much longer I'll be able to resist him when I want to do more myself."

"Mia, think about things before you go too far. Like you told me many times, once it's done, there's no going back."

"I know, Vic. I know."

"Are you seeing him tonight?"

"Yeah. We're going bowling and then to get something to eat. I think we might go back to his house to watch a movie. His parents are away."

"Oh, boy," Vicky said. "How about that for temptation!"

Miabella looked at her friend and sighed. "Yeah. How about that!"

* * *

Three hours later, the phone rang as Miabella tried on an outfit for her date with Alex. "Hi Al," she said, breathing into the phone, while she pulled a sweater over her head.

"Whatcha doing?" he asked.

"I'm figuring out a comfortable outfit for tonight."

"It doesn't matter what you wear because you always look great. Besides, I've never seen you any other way," Alex said, letting out a mischievous laugh as he spoke.

"Stop teasing me, Al. You know the sex thing's hard for me."

"Yeah, for me too. Holding back when I'm with you is torture."

"Thanks for being patient. I know you can have any girl you want and you're waiting around for me," Miabella said, apologizing for her old-fashioned ways.

"But you're the *only* girl I want."

"Alex! If I didn't know you better, that sounds like a line to get a girl to cave in."

"No, Mia. I *really really* care about you," he continued.

"I believe you, Al, but I'm not ready yet. Aren't things pretty good the way they are?"

"Yeah, I guess." Mia didn't know quite how to react to his answer. Alex broke the silence. "Let me go and get ready. I'll pick you up in an hour."

"Great, Al. I can't wait."

* * *

Around seven o'clock, Miabella's mom yelled up to her room. "Mia, Alex is here."

"Okay, mom. Tell him I'll be right down," she shouted from upstairs. Miabella walked down the right-hand side of the double winding staircase that adorned her family's center-hall colonial home. She dressed casually—a pair of black jeans with a lightweight, tan button-down sweater that accentuated her full breasts. Alex couldn't help but stare at her as she pranced down the regal staircase. *Wow, she's so beautiful! How did I get a girl like Mia?*

Miabella's parents entered the foyer. Alex walked over to Mr. Maxima and shook his hand. He kissed

Mrs. Maxima on the cheek, and then they exchanged goodbyes. Alex and Miabella walked out the cherry-wood front door, down the grey stone steps, and then headed for his jeep. As he closed the rickety door for his girlfriend, his mind wandered. *Miabella's family has money, yet she doesn't act like a spoiled, rich princess. She never makes me feel like I'm not good enough for her, unlike other girls. I care about her, but no sex frustrates me!* Alex decided to forget about it for now and enjoy his time with his girl.

At the bowling alley, Miabella threw more strikes than Alex. She noticed him staring at her backside, which stood out in her tight black jeans. "What's the matter, Al? Your game's off tonight. I'm beating you for a change." Miabella focused Alex's attention to the digital scoreboard, pointing to her score of 144 and his score of 132.

"I'm letting you win," he boasted. Alex planted a feather-soft kiss on Miabella's lips, sending rippling sensations down her back.

"Nice excuse," she said. *Oh boy. I'm already feeling nervous about tonight.*

"When we wrap up the game, is Paulie's Pizza okay?" Alex asked.

"Sure. I'm kind of hungry." Mia gave Alex a quick kiss on his cheek and began to bowl her last frame. She scored a 168 and Alex a 152. "I would've made a bet with you if I'd known I'd win. If—a little word that means so much," Mia said, in her typical theatrical style.

"You're right as usual . . . and beautiful too."

* * *

At 10:30, Alex's car pulled up to the front of the aqua-colored cape cod he lived in with his parents. The house had a single garage, which held his mother's car. Alex and his dad took turns parking in the short driveway leading to the garage. That night, Alex would park on the street so his parents could use the driveway to unload their suitcases early the next morning when they returned from their overnight trip.

Miabella didn't have to be home until 2:00. Alex kept wondering how the night would go because they had the house to themselves. *Should I be more aggressive with Mia, or would that scare her away? Will she become demanding if she sleeps with me?* Alex felt conflicted. He slid a DVD into the player. He had rented *The Great Gatsby*, a movie Miabella wanted to see but they had missed at the theaters. They both read the novel by F. Scott Fitzgerald in English Lit. Star-struck Miabella loved Leonardo DiCaprio, who played the lead male actor in the modern-day movie version of the classic novel. Alex also bought a giant carton of buttered popcorn to share with Mia.

Miabella held the popcorn carton on her lap, while Alex wrapped his free arm behind her shoulders and feasted on the buttery snack. The movie didn't do much for Alex, but Miabella appeared mesmerized by DiCaprio's portrayal of Gatsby. When she watched a movie, she became engrossed in the storyline. Alex would occasionally try to talk to Mia about the day's events, but she would just answer with "shush," pointing her delicate little finger over her smooth, full lips. Frustrated, Alex withdrew his arm from Miabella's back and started kissing the back of her neck.

"Al, I really want to see this," Miabella pleaded, while gently pulling away from Alex.

"Yeah, go ahead. Watch it," he said, as his lips moved from the back of her neck to her ear. His voice sounded sexier than usual to Miabella, and she began to feel that incredible tingly sensation that took over her body when Alex touched her.

"Al, come on. Do you think I can get into this movie with you doing that?"

"That's up to you. We can always watch it another night." Alex kissed Miabella's cheek, making his way to her lips.

Miabella couldn't take it anymore. She tried crossing her legs to suppress the feeling, but it did no good whatsoever. Alex looked at Mia, smiling with his seductive eyes, realizing how his kisses were affecting her. Then, Miabella surprised herself. She pulled away from Alex and placed the popcorn carton on the end table next to the sofa. She leaned in to kiss him, passionately thrusting her tongue into his welcoming mouth. They kissed for several minutes, when Alex pulled away from Miabella and looked into her eyes. "I love you, Mia," he said, with a look of deep sincerity.

Miabella thought she'd start shedding tears of happiness. She didn't know how to handle her feelings. She kissed him with a greater intensity than a small child enjoying her favorite ice cream cone in the summer heat. It took a few minutes for her to come up for air and stare into Alex's eyes. "I love you too," she said.

They continued kissing as Alex leaned Miabella back onto the sofa. When he got on top of her, she wrestled with her thoughts. *OMG, is this really happening? What if things go too far?* Alex knew Miabella well enough to take the time to talk to her, even in the heat of the moment. As he unbuttoned her sweater, he spoke softly. "Are you okay with this, Mia, or am I moving too fast?" Miabella stared into Alex's beautiful, captivating eyes. She didn't answer, but Alex came to the rescue, "I can't help it. You really turn me on," he said.

"I want you, Al, but there's no going back for me. I promised that I'd save myself for the guy I married."

"Mia, I'll never find a girl like you. You know that. I adore you. Not only am I so unbelievably attracted to you, but I love that you're such a good person. I won't hurt you."

"Oh, Al," Miabella sighed. "Let's see what happens." She unbuttoned the rest of her sweater to reveal a white lace bra. *I can't believe I'm doing this, but boy does it feel right.* Lowering her eyes, she unfastened the clasp that held her bra together in the front. She took Alex's hand and placed it on her breast. Alex caressed Miabella's breast with his hand as he removed her sweater and bra. He took off his T-shirt to reveal a muscular, well-groomed chest. Miabella felt safe with him on top of her, his clammy skin touching hers. At that moment, no one else in the world mattered.

Each time Alex removed a piece of Miabella's clothing, he looked to her for reassurance. The needle on the moral compass in her head moved frantically back and forth, like a flickering light bulb about to burn out. She felt a slight pounding between her eyebrows. *I hope I'm doing the right thing. I love him, and I know he loves me.*

Once they were both naked, Alex asked, "Mia. Are you sure about this?"

Mia's genuine smile expressed her deep love for Alex. The thoughts that circled around in her brain stopped, and the compass disappeared, replaced by a bright, comforting glow that lit the dim, unfamiliar corners of her mind. Miabella felt certain about her decision to sleep with Alex. "Yes, Alex," she answered, with a confident tone. "I love you so much. I'm ready."

"Oh, Mia," he responded, as he kissed the nape of her neck, gently rolling his tongue on her skin. But Alex had his own insecurities. Even though he loved Miabella with all of his heart and hoped to marry her in the future, he struggled with trusting women. His former girlfriend, Kara, had been unfaithful to him. Kara had the upper hand in their relationship, having slept with several guys before Alex started seeing her. She exuded sexual confidence, whereas Alex just began learning how to please a woman. His previous hookups happened while drinking, and he went through the motions. *What if Mia decides to move on too, like Kara? I'd be stupid not to notice how other guys gawk at her. Can I make her happy? With her family's wealth, Mia could have whatever she wants. What if I can't afford her lifestyle?* Alex stopped kissing Miabella and looked to her for reassurance.

"What's wrong?" she asked him.

"Nothing, Mia. I have to get a condom from my wallet." He would never want Mia to know he felt unsure of her love for him.

"Okay," Miabella said, as she breathed in some air. Now she had to be patient. Her heart thumped like it did before cheering tryouts, and her head felt like it would explode.

When Alex made love to Miabella, their eyes locked, pulling their faces and bodies toward each other like a needle to a magnet. The night would be engrained in their minds forever. Miabella felt Alex's love for her, and Alex didn't want to be anywhere else. They lay together, naked, for some time. Mia felt amazing until they began to put on their clothes. Then, those taunting thoughts resurfaced. *OMG, did I really do it? What if things don't work out for us?* Miabella tried to push the nagging thoughts away, but each time she put on another piece of clothing, she felt confused. Alex seemed unusually quiet. Once they were both dressed, he turned on *Saturday Night Live* for some comic relief. They'd watch the rest of *The Great Gatsby* another night. Cuddled together on the sofa, they didn't say anything.

Around 1:45, Alex and Miabella left, headed for her house. He walked her to the front door of the huge colonial, thinking how hard it would be to give her the things she deserved. Miabella wondered how she'd be able to face her parents without her eyes and body language revealing that something magical, yet confusing, had happened to her. But when Alex kissed her goodnight on her forehead and then her lips, she felt much better. She didn't want him to leave, but he had to wake up early for work the next day. Miabella watched Alex as he jumped into his jeep, threw a goodbye kiss with his hand, and drove away.

When Mia tried to fall asleep, she tossed and turned, dealing with a mixture of emotions. *Will Alex ask me to marry him in a few years? Does he love me enough to stay with me until we're both ready for marriage?* Hopeful for a future with Alex, Mia said her prayers and dozed off a few hours later.

* * *

Chapter Two

Miabella's Mistake?

At 7 o'clock the next morning, Miabella sent a text to Vicky: "Call my cell ASAP." Her nervous fingers banged out the text like a marathon runner approaching the finish line. She had promised to go to the mall with Vicky and Joe Carson, a neighbor and close friend. Mia grew up with Joe, and she thought of him like the big brother she never had. Yet, she didn't feel comfortable talking with

Vicky about her night with Alex in front of Joe. She needed to reach Vicky before the three of them got together. Within seconds, Vicky texted back, "Sorry, Mia, but I have to help my mom clean my grandma's place. Gotta go. Say hi to Joe for me." Miabella sighed. She texted back, "It's okay, Vic. I'll talk to you later." The conversation would have to wait.

At breakfast, Miabella forced herself to eat a whole wheat bagel and drink some orange juice while her mom cleaned the island countertop. She glanced at her mother. *What would she say about my night with Alex?* Mia could talk to her about almost anything, except sex. Worried that her mom would sense a difference in her, Mia struck up a quick conversation to avoid talking about her date.

"I think I'm going to the mall with Joe," Miabella said. "Vicky's mom needs her help with something, so she can't come with us." Mia rinsed her glass and plate and placed them in the dishwasher, trying to get out of the kitchen as fast as possible. "I guess I'll call Joe and see if he still wants to go."

"All right, but I barely get to talk to you these days," her mom said. "I'll see you later."

While walking up the staircase to her bedroom, Miabella scrolled down to Joe's number on her cell phone and placed a call. "Hi Joe. Do you still want to go to the mall this morning? Vicky can't make it."

"Sure," he replied. "Do you want me to pick you up?"

"No thanks. I'll meet you there because I'll probably visit Alex at work later on," Miabella answered.

"Okay, I'll be at the Gap getting some new T-shirts. See you there in an hour."

"That's perfect. Bye."

* * *

Joe and Miabella met at the Gap at the Fairway Mall at 11 o'clock. He had a bunch of T-shirts and jeans draped over his arm. Mia found a few pairs of faded jeans with torn knees. She tried them on because they were on sale and she wanted a pair with rips. "Boy, trying on all these jeans makes me tired," Miabella said.

"Not me," Joe said. "It makes me hungry."

After they made their purchases, they went to the Wendy's at the food court for burgers and fries. They went outside to sit on one of the wooden benches to enjoy their dessert in the beautiful sunshine. Miabella thought Joe seemed a little distant and less cheerful than usual. He usually devoured his yogurt in a few minutes; she noticed him twirling the half-eaten, melted yogurt with his spoon. When she chatted with him, he glanced away. For a few minutes, neither of them spoke. Miabella's mind kept wandering as thoughts of her night with Alex both excited and scared her.

Joe broke the silence. "Is there something on your mind?"

"I was going to ask you the same thing," she said. "You seem distant."

"Just things . . . things I've been thinking about."

"Like what? Talk to me," she said, as she nudged his arm.

What happened next took Miabella totally by surprise. Joe leaned over and gave her a passionate kiss on her lips. She pulled away and stared at him, not knowing what to say. Joe took her reaction as a green light, so he tried to kiss her again, until Miabella objected. "Joe, what are you doing?" she asked. "You know I'm with Al. Plus, you're like a brother to me."

"I'm sorry Mia, but that's what I've been thinking about. Lately, as I see you getting closer to Alex, I've realized that my feelings for you go beyond friendship. I always thought you were beautiful, but now I'm thinking about you all the time. I had to kiss you. I had to try, or I knew I would definitely regret it down the line."

"Joe, you're a great guy. We've been good friends

for so long, and I don't want to hurt you, but I'm crazy about Alex."

"Tell me, Mia. Kissing me . . . did it do anything at all for you?"

Miabella shook her head from right to left a few times, but her eyes and facial expressions said all Joe needed to hear. Yet, he didn't regret trying because he admired Miabella's special qualities. "Okay," he said. "Now I've made a complete ass of myself."

"No, no," Miabella said. "It's all right. We can pretend it never happened. It can stay between the two of us. Things won't change."

"Thanks, Mia, but if he ever hurts you, and you want to try with me . . ."

"I'll keep that in mind, but things are great with Al, and I'd never want to risk screwing up our friendship."

Little did Miabella know that while Joe kissed her, one of Alex's close friends, John Steel, walked by. Neither Miabella nor Joe noticed him looking at them. As Alex's closest friend, John felt compelled to tell him about what he witnessed. *But how?* He didn't want to just send a text or call because Alex would need his support; it would be better to tell him in person. John decided to wait for Alex outside of the AT&T store until his shift ended. He knew his friend would take the news hard. As he walked around the crowded mall, he wiped the sweat from his brows, aware that the perspiration had more to do with his nerves than the temperature.

Meanwhile, Miabella said goodbye to Joe and headed toward the AT&T store to visit Alex. An ear-to-ear smile beamed on his face when he saw his girlfriend. He motioned to her that he needed to help a customer. Miabella held up her cell phone and motioned to him to call her later. They had plans to see each other that night—hopefully to watch *The Great Gatsby*. Ironically, Alex's parents extended their trip for two more days, so Alex and Mia would have the house to themselves again. Too busy to talk to Mia, Alex shrugged his shoulders apologetically. Miabella left the store, satisfied with the few minutes she got to see her guy.

At five o'clock, John Steel walked over to the AT&T store. He waited for Alex at the entrance. Alex ended his day at 5:15 after his replacement arrived. Seeing John at the doorway surprised him. "Hey, Steel," he said. "Whatcha doing here?"

"Hey, man. I got something to talk to you about. It's pretty important."

"Okay, spill," Alex said, concerned.

"Let's go to my car first," John responded.

"Okay. Why so serious?" They walked in silence for a few seconds until they reached Steel's car. John sat in the driver's seat of his Honda, and Alex tiredly plopped himself down on the passenger side. Alex waited for his friend to talk.

"Al," he said. "I don't know how to tell you about what I saw a few hours ago."

"Just say it, that's all."

"It's something that's gonna rip you apart."

"Now you got me nervous. What is it, Steel? You know me well enough to realize I can handle a lot. My life's not been easy."

"I know," said John. "This is tough, though." He glanced at Alex. *Should I have ignored the whole incident? Miabella makes Alex happy, and she seems crazy about Al. But why would she kiss another guy? It doesn't make sense, but I did see it happen.* "Al, I saw Miabella earlier."

"Yeah. Me too, about a half hour ago."

"No, I mean a few hours ago."

"Yeah, she told me last night that she'd be at the mall today. She popped in to say hi, but I couldn't talk to her because a customer needed my help."

"Al, I mean . . . she wasn't alone."

"I know. Last night, she said she'd be shopping with Vicky."

"Well, not with Vicky, Al."

"What are you getting at?"

"I saw Mia with a guy—not anyone we know."

"And . . ."

"And they were kissing," John said, glancing away from Alex.

Alex felt like a brick hit his head. His mind raced. *Steel wouldn't lie to me, but I should trust Miabella. How could she kiss some guy after what we did last night?* Alex's insecurities resurfaced like a giant wave crashing toward a tranquil coastline. In the past, he had trusted Kara. He remembered how angry he'd been when he caught her cheating. After he confronted Kara, he learned that she had more sexual experience than he'd thought. But Miabella hadn't been with anyone else, and she didn't take their relationship lightly. *I don't know what to believe!* He turned toward John and said, "I gotta talk to her about this."

"Okay," John said. "Sorry to be the bearer of bad news."

"No, man. I would have told you too. I'll talk to you later."

"Bye, take care," John said, as he placed his hand on Alex's shoulder. He hated to see his friend upset.

Walking to his jeep, Alex stared at the ground. He drove home in a fog, overwhelmed with jealousy, trying to trust Miabella. *Maybe Steel saw her double at the mall.* Alex pictured Miabella's pretty face. *Maybe the guys are right. Is Mia too "high reach" for me because she's so beautiful and her family has money?* Whenever Alex talked to Steel about his insecurities, John said to ignore the guys because he could tell how much Mia cared for him. But Alex needed answers, even though he feared what he might hear. He couldn't wait to talk to Miabella in person, so he called her cell as soon as he got to his bedroom.

"Hey, Mia." Alex's voice sounded strained, or tired.

"Hi, Alex. I can't wait to see you tonight. I'm getting my clothes ready."

Alex ignored her comment. "I gotta talk to you about something."

"Okay, what's up?"

"What did you do today?"

"You know what I did. I went to the mall." The intensity in Alex's voice confused Mia.

"With who?"

"Why all the questions?" For the first time, Miabella felt uncomfortable talking with Alex, and she hated the feeling.

"Did you go to the mall with Vicky?" Alex raised his voice in an angry tone that she hadn't heard from him before that moment.

"No. She had to help her mom with something," Miabella responded, wondering about Alex's interrogation.

"So you went alone?"

"Not exactly. I went with a friend. Why are you being so weird?"

"Yeah . . . And friends kiss?"

Alex's bitter voice stung deep in her heart. Miabella pictured his beautiful, intense brown eyes turning to fiery rings of coal, piercing her through the phone. She froze. She got choked up, and her heart started racing. *OMG, who saw Joe kiss me? How was I supposed to react to my long-time friend kissing me? I pulled away before Joe's lips could touch mine a second time.* "I can explain, Al."

"Answer me," he yelled. "Were you kissing a guy at the mall?"

"Well . . . sort of. But he's not just some guy I hooked up with."

A flood of mixed feelings filled Alex's body as he tried not to scream at the girl he loved so passionately. "Mia, I thought you were different. You know how I feel about cheating, especially after Kara."

"Alex, he's just a friend. Please let me tell you what happened."

"You didn't even try to deny it, Mia. Nothing you can say will change this. You let him kiss you."

"No, Alex. He kissed me."

"I don't want to hear anymore. Goodbye, Mia."

"Alex, please let me explain," she cried. But Alex ended the call before Miabella could explain the circumstances behind the kiss. Miabella sat on the edge of her bed in disbelief. *How could he talk to me like that? Why didn't he let me explain? I never pictured Alex to be a jealous, angry boyfriend. If he loved me, why didn't he believe me—that I didn't kiss Joe?* Tears ran down Miabella's cheeks for what seemed like hours when Vicky called her cell.

"Hi, Mia. What's going on?" Vicky asked. Then she heard the sobbing on the other end. "What's wrong?"

"Oh, Vic. I had a huge fight with Alex."

"Are you kidding? I thought things were going great?"

"They were, but something happened today that changed everything." And Miabella told Vicky about Joe, and the surprise kiss, and his confession about his feelings for her, and the shocking way Alex treated her.

"Look, Mia. He shouldn't treat you like that. You're a good person and a faithful girlfriend. What now?"

"Vic, I need to think about this. My head's so confused."

"Mia, do you want to go to Starbucks, get some coffee, and talk about how to handle this?"

"No. I need to be alone tonight. Thanks anyway."

"Are you sure?"

"Yeah, Vic."

"All right. Call me anytime you want. Please try not to cry all night. Things will work out. He's lucky to have a girl like you."

"And I'm lucky to have a friend like you. Bye."

"Bye."

Miabella always felt better after talking to Vicky. Everything happened so quickly that she didn't get a chance to tell her that she slept with Alex, or to talk with her about the different emotions she felt. But Miabella needed time to herself to figure it all out. *How can I get Alex to listen to me? Should I try to see him in person? I feel confused and nervous about this dark side of him.*

Miabella spent the evening listening to music, alone. She didn't get much sleep, but when she woke up at 6 a.m., she figured out what she needed to do. She never lacked for words when she wrote in the privacy of her bedroom, so she'd reach out to Alex through her writing. Miabella wrote a loving, apologetic letter, explaining her friendship with Joe and her dedication to Alex.

Dear Alex,

I often think about that warm September day we first met on WP's campus. You totally won me over with your charm and good looks. I saw in your eyes a kindness that's missing in so many people I meet. As I got to know you better, I realized how much I loved everything about you.

Please believe me when I say that I didn't respond to Joe's kisses. How could I want to kiss anyone but you, especially after our intimate night? As long as I live, I will never forget the passion I felt for you. I never imagined that any guy would make me want to give in to my desires and go against my morality. Somehow, it seemed natural and pure to be with you.

Just to clear things up, Joe's been my friend since I was two years old. I consider him the big brother I never had, and it shocked me when he kissed me. I planned on telling you some time in the near future, but it didn't seem right to bring it up after the beautiful night we had. When Joe kissed me, I didn't cause a scene because I didn't want to hurt or humiliate him. Instead, I explained how much I care about you and told him to move on with his life. I don't know if Joe knew what he was doing when he kissed me anyway. He only thought he had romantic feelings for me after he realized how deeply I care about you. Maybe in some weird way he had a brotherly interest to protect me, and he confused his emotions.

I promised Joe that I wouldn't tell anyone about him kissing me because he feels embarrassed. Please forget it *ever happened, like Joe and I agreed to forget. I know John has your best interests at heart, and I don't blame him for telling you about what he saw. Maybe you can show him my letter so that he also understands what happened, and you don't have to feel humiliated. Hopefully, John didn't tell anyone else. I don't want to hurt Joe because he truly is a good guy.*

Alex, when we spoke on the phone, the angry tone of your voice frightened me, and I might not have reacted the way I should have. Maybe I needed to reassure you more about how much I love you. Maybe I would have jumped to conclusions too if one of my friends saw you kissing a girl.

I decided to write to you instead of calling because you can't hang up on a letter. If I tried to talk to you in person, I might not have been able to express everything I wanted to say without you screaming again. Alex, I know we all have a dark side, but it hurt me deeply to hear your attacking words.

I hope that you read my letter and don't tear it up and throw it away. I wanted to give you a chance to hear my explanation, accept my apology, and think about our future. I still love you, and I still want to be your girlfriend. Remember that I'm hurting too. Please understand. The decision is yours.

With all of my love,

Miabella

After Miabella finished writing the letter, she threw on a pair of jeans and a T-shirt, brushed her teeth, and washed her face. When she looked in the mirror, she saw the effects of her argument with Alex. Her bloodshot, puffy eyes and swollen cheeks looked awful. Like a numb robot, she sprayed Alex's favorite perfume on the letter, placed it in an envelope, wrote his name and address on the front, affixed her return address sticker, and stuck on a stamp. Then she walked to the civic center down the street from her house. She stopped at the mailbox and took the letter out of her purse. Before she put it down the postal chute, she held it to her chest, took a deep breath, and looked up to the heavens. While walking home, she reflected on the warm, sunny weather that sharply contrasted with her mood. *How ironic!*

Chapter Three

Miabella's Future

The Monday morning after Miabella mailed her letter to Alex, the weather paralleled her solemn mood. She stared out her bedroom window, watching the street sign bending backward and forward as the wind and rain pounded on it. Mia wondered if she'd done the right thing. *Would it have been better to take a drive to Alex's house and talk to him face-to-face?* She wasn't sure, but she felt that *the Alex she knew* would react positively to her heartfelt, apologetic words. Time would tell.

Over the next few days, Miabella functioned, despite her depressed state. She attended classes but found it difficult to focus. Instead of doing her homework at the library, she rushed home to her bedroom and wept over her textbooks, drying away the warm tears with her shaky hand. Mia covered her swollen eyelids with extra makeup so her parents wouldn't notice. She wasn't ready to tell them about the breakup. They would be angry with Alex for hurting her.

Eventually, Miabella invited Vicky to her house and told her about her night with Alex before the breakup. Mia expected Vicky to be angry with Alex. "You mean he had the nerve to treat you like that after you slept with him," Vicky said in her high-pitched voice, expressing disbelief. "He knew how much that meant to you. The least he could do is give you a call and talk with you after you sent him that letter."

"I know, Vic. That's what I've been thinking. I'll give him a few days to cool down. He'll come around, I guess."

"I hope so. If that's what you still want. He has to learn to trust you more. I wouldn't want to be with someone who acts like that. Wow, for a good-looking guy, he sure is insecure."

"Yeah, but so am I sometimes. And my pride won't let me go crawling back for forgiveness. I made a sincere attempt to fix things; now it's up to him."

Before she left the Maxima house, Vicky gave Miabella a warm hug and said, "Good luck, girl. You know I'm here for you."

* * *

One week passed and still no word from Alex. *He* needed to reach out to *her* now. On her way to the parking garage at WP, Miabella spotted a couple. The guy looked a lot like Alex. In fact, *it was Alex*. She recognized his shirt—a plaid polo she had given him for his birthday. A pretty bleached blonde with an incredible figure stood next to Alex. Mia recognized her from last semester's English class. *That girl! I never liked the way she looked at Alex whenever he'd walk me to class and kiss me goodbye.* Miabella managed to hide behind an old Volkswagen to listen to their conversation.

"Yeah, but I'm over her," Miabella heard Alex say to the blonde.

"Are you sure? You guys looked pretty close the last time I saw you in front of Dr. Harvey's English classroom," she said. "What happened?"

"I don't want to talk about it," Alex snapped, defensively.

"That's cool," she said, choosing her words carefully. "I'm happy I have you all to myself."

Miabella started to shake all over. She lost her balance and almost fell onto the concrete garage floor. Alex pulled the blonde in close to him, embraced her, and kissed her—not a short kiss on the lips, but what appeared to be a lengthy, deep kiss. She rubbed up against him, and the two were getting heated, when Miabella decided she had enough. She crept along the edge of the Volkswagen until she reached her car, making sure that neither of them noticed her.

Miabella drove toward the exit at the back of the parking garage, far from Alex's view. She cried the whole way home. *How could Alex do this to me? What a slap in the face! Instead of trying to work things out with me, he hooks up with that sexy blonde. How much could he have loved me if he moved on so quickly? Do I really know Alex?*

When she arrived at her house, Miabella dried the tears from her eyes and headed for her room. She didn't want her mom to see her crying because she wasn't up to answering all kinds of questions. She managed to avoid Mrs. Maxima by yelling from the top of the staircase, "Mom, I'm home. I'll have my dinner later. I need to talk with a classmate about a group project." She tossed off her flip-flops and threw herself back on her bed.

Miabella called Vicky, happy to hear a genuine voice. She sobbed uncontrollably, giving Vicky the details of the display of affection she saw between her ex and that blonde. Vicky expressed her disgust. "That sucks," she said angrily. "How could he move on so quickly?"

Vicky told Miabella to come to her house later and to bring her pajamas. She planned to invite a few of their friends to spend the night, watching movies and eating cookies and ice cream. It would be good therapy for Miabella. Vicky reassured Mia that she'd find the right guy and that being a virgin didn't matter much. Miabella had been a rarity, but she still had good values and much to offer a decent guy.

Little did Miabella know that her letter never reached Alex. On that sunny Sunday morning when she went to the postal box, she couldn't foresee that a torrential storm on the following day would cause the mail carrier to lose her letter down the sewer.

Chapter Four

Rich Marvice's Nightmares

uring the daytime while delivering mail on his route in Caldwell, Rich Marvice smiled as he passed familiar faces and whistled his favorite Pharrell Williams' song, "Happy." He enjoyed the mild, sunny days and felt blessed to be working outdoors. But nighttime brought sadness into his cheery life. Rich mumbled in his sleep as he tossed and turned. His wife wondered what troubled her husband. Rich eventually decided to talk to her about the terrible gust of wind that caused him to be irresponsible the first day on the job.

"Aggie, I've been tormented by something for a few weeks now," Rich said.

"What is it, hon?" she asked. "You haven't been sleeping soundly, but I figured you felt pressured adjusting to your new job, especially after months of unemployment."

"Ag, everyone at the post office treats me great, and I love my route. I couldn't be happier with my job, especially in weather like we've been having. Ask me again in July and August, when I'm dealing with the heat, and I might not answer the same," he chuckled.

"Then, what is it, Rich?"

"Something happened on my first morning of work, and I didn't handle it properly. And it's been bugging me for some time. I'm having awful nightmares too."

"Talk to me, hon." Aggie waited to hear his story.

"Remember my first day?" he asked.

"I remember. I felt horrible that you had to deal with heavy wind and rain your first day on the job."

"Ag, that day was a blessing and a curse. The wind whipped against me, and the rain stung as it touched my face! At the civic center, I opened the postal box and started to place a batch of letters in my bag when a strong gust of wind caused me to drop the mail. Once I gained my footage, I noticed that three letters escaped my hands and headed down a stream of water toward the sewer. I rushed to grab them, when another strong blast of wind knocked me to my knees. By the time I reached for the letters, they went into the sewer, out of my sight."

"Oh, boy," Aggie said. "How upsetting!"

"Feeling bewildered and incompetent, I forced myself to forget about the incident instead of reporting it to my supervisor because I didn't want to risk being fired my first day on the job. Days later, the guilt ate at me. Maybe my boss could have talked to someone from the sewer department and retrieved the letters."

"Don't worry so much, Rich. With that much rain they probably ended up illegible," Aggie reassured.

"You're always my rock, Ag."

"Rich, you can't sleep at night because you feel guilty for not telling your supervisor about the letters?"

"Partly. You know how I feel about honesty. But I had to put you and Jack first. I couldn't afford to lose this job with you out of work, home with our son."

"But why didn't you talk to me sooner?"

"You had enough on your hands taking care of a newborn. I didn't want to add more stress to your life."

Aggie placed her arm on her husband's shoulder, looked into his sad eyes, and gave him a quick yet comforting kiss on his lips. "You can talk to me any time, hon. I get the feeling that something else is bothering you."

Rich took a minute to clear his throat before he spoke. "I can't stop thinking about the people who sent those letters. Who were they intended for? What were they about? What if the loss of those letters—

even just one of the three—had a terrible affect on someone's life? I couldn't live with myself."

"Relax, Rich. You're too good. I'm sure that those letters didn't involve anything monumental. Maybe they were three household bills, and the worst thing that happened is that the electric company turned off someone's power."

"See what I mean, Ag. And that's one of the better scenarios because at least that person could pay the bills and fix things. What if, for some reason, those letters were meant to change someone's life?"

"Oh, Richie. Stop worrying. You can't go back in time. And you can't keep wondering about the letters that were lost. God will take care of that."

Rich kissed his wife's forehead. That night, he slept peacefully, knowing his wife and God were on his side. He would never know about Miabella Maxima, and how the lost letter to Alex might have changed their relationship and her future. He would never know all three letters did not belong to one person. And he would never understand how the lives of Laura Spelling and Jonathan Wright would be impacted by their lost correspondence as well.

Chapter Five

Laura Spelling's Plea

*L*aura Spelling and her son Derek faced a difficult future. When Laura's husband Mark died suddenly of a heart attack, everything changed. Derek battled depression for months, telling his mom he couldn't feel happy without his father in his life. Laura struggled with her own feelings but tried to keep positive for her sixteen-year-old son, the most important person in the world to her.

Derek, an only child, idolized his dad. The two often spent Saturday mornings together, driving golf balls, fishing, or checking out new construction in the area. Sometimes, they would get up at 6 a.m., stop for a bagel and a cup of coffee, and then head for Wantage in northern New Jersey, about an hour drive from Caldwell. Mark's friend Travis lived there, and he had access to spots that were great for fishing. The three men would fish for hours. When Mark and Derek returned home, suntanned and excited, they shared details about their day with Laura. Although she never understood the lure of fishing, she enjoyed hearing about how they would catch a fish and return it to the water. She felt blessed that her husband was a good father and shared a special bond with their son.

After Mark's death on that gloomy April morning, Derek realized he lost his closest friend. Although he had many friends—his baseball teammates and guys he worked with at the Apple computer store—he valued his relationship with his dad. Derek felt safe with his father because Mark never judged him. His friends often made comments about how boring it must be to spend time with his father, but he would laugh it off. Although one would never know it when Derek hung out with his friends—playing video games and acting goofy—his maturity surpassed his years.

Derek couldn't help but compare his father to the fathers of his close friends, who were self-absorbed and often absent in their children's lives. Mark managed to attend every one of Derek's baseball games, even if only for the last few innings. Tears filled Derek's eyes whenever he recalled his father hastily parking his blue Toyota in the school lot, outside of the white-painted lines, before running to the field to watch him play ball. Derek wondered if he could handle his senior year of baseball without his father's presence and support.

Yet, he had a supportive, selfless mother. Over the years, Laura kept their family together like glue sealed an envelope. She worked part-time as a teaching assistant, cooked fabulous meals, and made sure her husband and son had everything they needed.

However, Laura regretted not being able to give Derek a brother or a sister. Because she and Mark were older, adoption didn't seem feasible. After Laura had several miscarriages, the couple decided that Derek would be their only child. Yes, they pampered him, but he deserved it because he was a special, loving son with a bright future.

With their extended family living in Nevada—thousands of miles away from Caldwell—Laura and Derek relied on each other for comfort. The Spellings had left Nevada and started a new life apart from their relatives because of Mark's job. Mark's supervisor had offered him a more lucrative position at PSE&G, but he had to relocate to New Jersey. Although Mark had a successful career as an engineer, if he accepted the promotion to Engineering Department Supervisor, it would mean more money for his family. Since Derek was an honor student and a talented athlete, he stood a good chance of being accepted to an Ivy League university, and tuition would be costly. Mark's new position at PSE&G would assure that he could provide the money for expenses not covered by scholarships. After they considered the advantages, all three agreed they'd move to Caldwell.

In time, the Spellings adjusted to their fast-paced New Jersey lifestyle and enjoyed their new home, until that fateful spring morning. Mark had a weird sensation in his chest, got up from the breakfast table to continue getting ready for work, but passed out before he could leave. Derek started CPR as Laura telephoned 911 for help, but Mark died seconds before the ambulance arrived. The next few days were surreal, as Laura and Derek went through the rituals associated with a death and burial. Mark was only fifty years old when he died. He had life insurance and a solid investment portfolio, so Laura and Derek wouldn't struggle financially. Laura was a young widow—only forty-five. She couldn't imagine life without her husband, but she had to find the strength to move on—for Derek's sake.

Over the next few months, Laura managed to keep it together. Derek's happiness came first, and that meant helping him adjust to their new situation. He needed to remain positive so that he could finish high school and enjoy the college experience he looked forward to before Mark's death. Laura took exercise and art classes to fill her time. However, Derek had a tough time during baseball season. Ball games proved challenging without Mark's presence and support. But Laura would say, "You know your father's cheering for you, Derek. Make him proud." And Derek would perform to the best of his ability, in memory of his dad, who had worked with him on hitting and throwing for years in their back yard and at the school's baseball field. At the end of the season when the coaches highlighted each team member's efforts, Derek ranked second in terms of batting averages. He could see his father's smiling face in the clouds as he gazed at the sky.

That summer, Laura and Derek visited their relatives in Nevada for a few weeks. Watching Derek laughing with his twin cousins, Pete and Jim, made Laura ecstatic. The boys formed a team and played volleyball with the neighbors in the pool. Like Derek, the twins were athletes, and the three neighbors couldn't beat them, but everyone had a great time. Pete and Jim were a few years younger than Derek, and they idolized him. At the airport, they promised to visit Derek at college once they got their driver's licenses.

* * *

One Saturday morning in early September, Derek talked to his mom about her upcoming birthday. He knew a birthday celebration without Mark would be difficult, so he wanted to do his best to make her day special. He also thought about the adjustment they'd have to make once he left for college. As he poured her a cup of coffee at the breakfast nook, he asked,

"Mom, what would you like to do for your forty-sixth birthday? You have me from now until 10:00 tonight. I just have to stop at the bank after breakfast."

"Anything would be fine, son. But don't feel you have to spend the entire day with me," Laura responded.

"I want to mom. How about taking a ride to Point Pleasant? We can bring our bikes. The weather is perfect for bike riding. And we'll have lunch, and then head home. Does that sound like a good idea, mom?"

"Yes. That sounds great. As long as I'm not interfering with your plans," Laura said. "And, by the way, why do you need to go to the bank? I don't want you spending any money on me. You can buy me a lobster dinner after you get your first full-time job. With perfect SAT scores, you should be accepted at some great colleges." Her proud smile lit up her face like a star at the top of a Christmas tree.

"I need to withdraw money for tonight because I'm going out with the guys when we get back," Derek answered. *It feels great to see Mom smile. She's been sad for so many months, but now she glows whenever she speaks about my future.*

After breakfast, Derek put their bikes in the back of Laura's Range Rover, while Laura got ready. As she applied her makeup, she thought about their bittersweet future. *I'm going to miss Derek, but he needs to be on his own. Saying goodbye to him at the dorm will be difficult, and going home to an empty house will feel strange. Maybe I'll take a leave of absence from my job and live in Nevada near Sarah during Derek's first semester. I wish Mark could share this experience with us. Even though Sarah offered to help us check into the dorm, I don't want to bother her. My sister has to take care of her own family.*

Derek poked his head into Laura's room and said, "Ok, mom. I'll be right back. I'll beep the horn." He went over to his mother, handed her a birthday card, and kissed her on the cheek.

"Thanks, Derek. I'll be ready," Laura said. She finished curling her auburn hair and went into the living room. She sat in Mark's brown leather recliner and read the card, hoping to share it with her husband. The words made her soft blue eyes fill with tears. Derek had written them himself inside a note card with a picture of a serene landscape.

Dear Mom,

As an only child, you know how close I've been to you and Dad. The hole in my heart is still there, but you help fill it up a little more each day. Getting through this past year has been incredibly hard for us, but I'm grateful we have each other. You are the best, mom. I love you. And, yes, I'll definitely miss you when I'm away at college.

I know I can't take Dad's place in your life, but I'll do my best to make sure you have a happy birthday.

With love,

Derek

Laura read the letter over again. *What a great son he turned out to be! I'll put the past behind me and share my birthday with Derek.* She turned on the television and waited for him to return.

Meanwhile, Derek drove to the PNC Bank to withdraw money so he could treat his mom for lunch and dinner. He parked the SUV across the street and walked toward the entrance, when he noticed a few police cars parked on the side street. Before he could place his fingers on the door handle, a man wearing a black baseball cap and face mask pushed into him. Officers tackled the man, yelling for Derek to get out of the way. In the scuffle, the robber's gun went off. The officers apprehended the robber, placed him in handcuffs, and read him his Miranda rights.

Derek felt a pain near his chest and dropped to his knees. As he looked down and grabbed it, he saw a red stain on his yellow T-shirt and felt blood gushing out, and he realized what happened. Someone leaning over Derek tried to stop the blood. "Hang in there, pal," the stranger said. Derek could only think about his mother and her birthday. He needed to get home to her, but he couldn't speak—not one word. In a dream-like state, he watched as two EMT workers placed him on a stretcher and put him in an ambulance, headed for Mountainside Hospital.

Derek's wallet held his driver's license with his photo ID, so the police were able to identify him. One of the hospital staff members found Laura's phone number as an ICE contact that read "mom," so she called, hoping to be of assistance. "Hello, my name is Sandra, and I'm calling from Mountainside Hospital," she said. "Are you the mother of Derek Spelling?"

A knot welled up in Laura's throat as she responded yes. She had a sickening feeling that something terrible happened.

The nurse continued. "Your son's at Mountainside. He's in surgery because of a gunshot wound."

"Oh my God," Laura cried. "Is he all right? Is he going to be okay?"

"I don't know, Mrs. Spelling."

"I'm on my way," Laura said, frantically. Laura felt a fever throughout her body like she experienced the day Mark had the heart attack. *Not my son too. Please, God, don't take Derek too.* She called her neighbor, Terry Hartlin, whom she had gotten closer to since Mark's passing.

"Hello," said Terry.

"Ter. . . Derek." Laura sobbed uncontrollably.

"What's the matter? What about Derek?"

"He's . . . He's been shot. Can you . . . take me to Mountainside Hos . . . Hospital?" Laura cried.

"Sure, right away. Meet me in my driveway," Terry said.

Chapter Six

The Spellings' Fate

At the hospital, Terry comforted Laura as they waited to hear about Derek's condition. "He's a fighter," she said. Terry paused to think of the right words to reassure her friend. "He'll do everything in his power to make it through."

"I keep praying he will," Laura mumbled, as her throat tightened, "but the ER doctor said he lost a lot of blood." She hated the thought of her son in a cold operating room, fighting for his life, with tubes attached to him.

"Let's not worry about the extent of his injuries. Let's keep praying for his recovery," Terry answered.

Laura's thoughts shifted to Derek's accomplishments. "Terry, it's not fair. Derek's such a good student, and he's excited about his future. If he makes it through, will he be okay to go away to college?"

"Let's pray for the best outcome," Terry said.

They waited on edge, hoping to hear some news. Laura watched the clock on the pale blue hospital wall, which stared back at her like a demon. Those pointy, knife-like hands taunted her, stealing more and more hours from her time with her son. She wanted to get up out of her chair and push those damn hands back to nine o'clock in the morning—before Derek left for the bank. If only she had insisted they leave right then, the robber wouldn't have shot Derek. She couldn't help but blame herself, even though she knew in her heart you can't control fate.

The more time passed, the more Laura twisted in her chair. Her forehead pounded to the beat of the old clock, and she could feel her heart thumping rapidly. Over the sound of her heartbeat, she heard footsteps. Her eyes shifted from that ominous clock to two doctors who approached her. "Are either of you women Mrs. Spelling?" the grey-haired, older physician asked.

"Yes, I am," Laura responded.

"Your son made it through surgery."

"Thank God," Laura rejoiced. She hugged the two doctors and thanked them repeatedly. But the concerned look on the older doctor's face frightened Terry.

The grey-haired doctor continued, "I must tell you that Derek's condition is critical due to the amount of blood loss. The bullet in his chest fragmented, and some of the fragments couldn't be removed. We'll have to monitor him closely over the next twenty-four hours."

"Does that mean he might not make it?" Laura cried.

"I wish I had better news. You can visit him, but he'll probably sleep a lot. I know it's difficult, but try to remain positive in his presence. If he talks, keep the conversations brief to conserve his energy." Then the two doctors walked out of the waiting room.

Laura and Terry went to the nurses' station to ask for Derek's room number. When Laura saw her handsome son with all sorts of tubes connected to him, she almost passed out. Terry grabbed her friend's arm to keep her from falling. They sat down in two chairs, side by side, and dozed off, drained from the stress. Meanwhile, nurses came in and out of the room, checking on Derek. Hours later, a low-sounding voice called out, "Mom."

Laura jumped out of her chair and ran to her son. She took his hand in hers. "Yes, Derek."

"Mom. The nurse said someone shot me. I don't feel so well."

Laura let out a little nervous laugh. "Of course, you don't. But you'll get stronger every day."

"Mom. I'm sorry I ruined your birthday."

"Are you kidding, Derek? I got my birthday gift when you pulled through surgery. We can celebrate once you're better."

"But mom. What if I don't make it?"

"Shush," Laura said. "Please rest. I'll be here until you're well enough to come home." She tenderly kissed her son's hand and watched his pale face light up with a smile. "I love you, son." Her voice cracked slightly.

"Me too, mom," he answered. And then Derek fell asleep again.

Although Laura felt content that Derek spoke to her, she got a nauseous feeling in the pit of her stomach; her son realized he could die. Since Laura intended to stay at the hospital, Terry planned to stay too. She didn't want to leave Laura alone, so she called her husband to explain what happened. Terry sat in the armchair beside her distraught friend, leaned over, and gave her a hug. Feeling helpless, they waited for Derek to recover.

After a few hours, the women fell asleep in the chairs until the sound of Derek's hospital monitor, indicating trouble, startled them. Within seconds, the staff rushed in and asked Laura and Terry to leave the room. Laura cried out, "Please, let me stay with my son." But the nurses insisted she leave while they tried to revive Derek. Reluctantly, the women waited outside the door. Laura's crying reminded Terry of the day Mark died. Terry didn't know what else to do but hug Laura. She feared the worst, as Laura did.

When the doctors told Laura that they weren't able to save Derek, she let out a piercing cry. It cut through everyone's ears and hearts sharper than a surgeon's tools. The agony of losing Mark only a year ago paled in comparison to the double loss she now faced. Her body shivered. Thoughts raced through her mind quicker than she could process them. *I found my inner strength to help Derek when Mark died, but how can I get through this? Do I want to?*

One of the nurses comforted Laura. With a low, soothing voice, she said, "Mrs. Spelling, take this card. The therapist specializes in grief counseling and is highly recommended by patients and doctors." Laura nodded a thank-you and tucked the business card in the outer pocket of her purse.

The grey-haired doctor placed his hand on her shoulder and said, "I'm sorry we couldn't save your son. The loss of such a young, healthy guy is disheartening."

Trembling and defeated, Laura longed for this day to be a terrible nightmare that would end when she woke up.

* * *

Laura's sister Sarah and her family flew in from Nevada to attend the services. When Laura saw her nephews Pete and Jim at the funeral, they looked like two kindergartners who lost their way home and didn't know which road to take. Sarah, whose effervescent smile lit up any room she entered, looked bewildered. Back at the house, she told Laura to stay with them in Nevada—at least until she could get herself together. Laura agreed to spend time with the only family she had left, but it would be tough saying goodbye to Terry, her closest, irreplaceable friend.

*   *   *

On the night before Laura's departure, she talked for hours with Terry. "Ter," she said, "I'll never forget how you were there for me at the lowest points in my life. I hope you understand why I need to spend some time in Nevada."

"Sure," Terry said. "I get it. But you won't be here for the trial. Don't you think it might help you move forward to get justice for Derek?"

"I thought about it, Ter. But I'm not strong enough to handle it. I'll leave it in the hands of the jury and God. At some point, I'll come back to go through Derek's belongings. I plan on selling the house and moving to Nevada. But I promise I'll visit you, and you're always welcome to visit me."

"I want what's best for you. If you'd like, I can fill you in about the trial. I plan on being there for part of the time."

"Thank you, Ter. You're truly an angel."

* * *

As the trial progressed, details about the young man who shot Derek began to unfold. Sixteen-year-old Louis Chalez had never been in trouble with the law and had never received a detention at his high school. By all accounts, Louis appeared to be a decent kid. Hard luck had fallen upon his family the weeks prior to the shooting. His father left his mother and their children for his mistress. Mrs. Chalez had to provide for a four-month-old little girl, in addition to Louis and three other siblings. The situation forced Louis to become a man overnight. He took on a second part-time job so he could help with the bills. He also watched his younger siblings during the hours Mrs. Chalez worked as a waitress on a night shift.

Still, with both of them working, they couldn't make ends meet. Mr. Chalez failed to pay several of the household bills during his last month with his family, so his wife had to put extra money out to ensure that the gas and electric wouldn't be turned off. He charged numerous items for his mistress on Mrs. Chalez's credit card, so she had to contend with an enormous bill and subsequent finance charges. As the days passed, she found herself deeper in debt as more of her husband's selfish behavior became apparent.

Louis's life unraveled before his eyes. He couldn't sleep well at night, tormented by weird dreams. In one nightmare, he pictured giant dice rolling against each other, as they pushed their way down a dollar-covered path toward the door of the small cottage-like edifice he called home. After each dream, he'd wake up in a pool of sweat, panicking over how he could make enough money to support his mother and siblings.

To add to his stress, junior year of high school was important to him because he would be taking the SATs, and his scores would affect his admission to colleges. Unfortunately, he could barely stay awake in class, let alone study for the SATs. One day, a classmate threw an eraser at his head to wake him up so that the teacher wouldn't get on Louis' back. After school, Louis would rush to his part-time job at the Burger Hut, where he worked from 3:30 until 6:30. Then, he went to his second job down the street at the local pharmacy, where he worked as a stock boy until 9 p.m.

As much as school challenged him, and his back-to-back jobs made him tired, nothing compared to the stress he felt caring for his siblings once his mother left for her waitress job at 10 p.m. Although the children went to bed at 9 o'clock, the youngest member of the family, Rosa, did not follow the plan. When Louis went to his bed for a much-needed night's sleep, Rosa would start wailing because she was hungry, or wet, or cranky. He rocked his little sister to sleep in his arms and watched the clock. *This is impossible! How will I be able to wake up at five to do my homework if I don't get some sleep?*

The difficulty Louis faced with his home situation and lack of sleep sparked a thought in his brain that grew into an out-of-character, irrational decision. Louis lived only minutes from Newark, where he heard he could purchase a gun. He planned to rob a bank in Caldwell, a fairly affluent town about twenty miles from his home. At first, he thought about taking a fake gun with him. After all, he didn't want to shoot anybody. Louis tried to justify his plan. *Banks have tons of money, so they won't miss a little of it. Someday, when I have extra cash, I'll make an anonymous donation to the bank.* In the end, he decided to buy a gun from a thug who knew one of his friends. He gave the guy $100—money he saved for an emergency—for the weapon.

On the night before Louis robbed the bank, Rosa cried more than usual because she started teething. Exhausted, he rocked her three separate times until she finally fell asleep. Louis tossed and tossed in his bed, unable to get comfortable. Confusing thoughts filled his head. *Am I crazy trying to rob a bank? What if I get caught?* When his father left their family and Louis stepped into his shoes, he pretended to his mother and his friends that he had things under control. In reality, he sizzled like a firecracker ready to ignite whenever a slight gust of wind blew his way.

At the trial, Louis' attorney revealed the details of the boy's sad life. Although the gun that killed Derek went off accidentally in the scuffle while the police moved in to arrest Louis, he still had to pay for his actions. Convicted of manslaughter and armed robbery, Louis would be going to prison for twenty years. The money he stole from the bank amounted to $455. Although it would have done little to help with his family's debt, it would have paid for food and baby formula.

*   *   *

After the trial ended, Terry had a long phone conversation with Laura about the verdict and the facts presented. Although Laura recovered at a slow pace, living with her relatives helped. She felt sad to leave the home she shared with Mark and Derek, but she needed to move to Nevada, where good memories gave her peace. Yet, Laura felt she needed closure, so she planned on visiting the boy who shot Derek when she returned to New Jersey.

When the cab pulled up in front of Laura's house in Caldwell, reminders of sad and happy times tore at her heart. Her legs and hands shook as she got out of the cab and tipped the driver. Laura headed for the front

door, luggage in hand. *I can do this. I need to do this.*
Before she turned the key, her faithful friend stood
beside her. "Terry. It's good to see you," Laura said, as
the two women embraced. "I've missed you."

"Me too," Terry said. "I'll come inside with you so
that you don't have to face this alone."

"Thank you so much."

In the days that followed, Terry helped Laura go
through Derek's belongings. Laura donated most of the
items to local charity. She gave special articles, such as
Derek's fishing pole, to Terry for her nephew. She'd
take Derek's trophies to his cousins in Nevada when
she returned. Laura also worked with a realtor to
determine a fair price for her house. Although parting
with her home would be tough, she knew she could
never live there without Mark and Derek.

Over a cup of coffee, Laura talked about how she
needed closure. She felt sorry for the boy who shot
Derek, but she needed to ask him why he didn't find
another way to help his family. His actions ruined two

young lives—his and Derek's—as well as two families. Laura took a deep breath and told Terry her plan. "Ter, I decided to write a letter to the boy who shot Derek to request a visit before I leave for Nevada. I hope he agrees to meet me because I have unanswered questions. I also want to tell him that I don't hate him, despite my grief."

"That's really kind of you, Laura. I don't think I could be so strong. But, like I told you, the boy seemed incredibly remorseful at the trial. I believe he didn't intend to kill anyone."

"I got that feeling when you told me the details. I've been talking to my therapist, trying to find peace."

"Still, you have every reason to be hateful."

"It's not like me to be hateful. I won't honor Derek's memory, or Mark's, if I don't forgive this boy and move on. He's paying for his mistake, and his mother must be suffering too."

*   *   *

The next evening, Laura wrote the letter—in memo style.

September 14, 2014

To: Louis Chalez

*From: Mrs. Laura Spelling (mother of
            Derek Spelling)*

Would you please agree to a visit from me before the end of the month since I will be permanently leaving New Jersey in a few weeks? I think it will help us both get closure. If you plan to meet with me, have your lawyer call my cell phone at (973) 709-0545.

Laura wrote the prison address on the envelope, sealed it, placed a return address sticker and a stamp on it, and took a walk to the civic center. She mailed the letter that evening at the postal box in front of the civic center instead of waiting to mail it at the post office the following morning. On one hand, she wanted to meet with Louis, face-to-face, and deal with her emotions. If he seemed remorseful, it might enable her to forgive him. Yet, another part of her didn't want to meet with Louis. *Can I handle talking to this kid? He killed my son.* By the time she arrived home, she felt more confused than ever. Laura said a prayer and asked God to guide her. If she heard from the boy's lawyer, she'd set up a meeting. If not, she'd leave for Nevada and start a new life.

* * *

Several weeks passed without a word from Louis' lawyer. Laura concluded that it must be too difficult for the boy to face her. Like a parent who intervenes to defend a child being bullied, God answered her prayer in a way that would inflict the least amount of pain. Deep down, Laura knew meeting with Louis would open wounds she struggled to keep closed. Pushing these thoughts aside, she continued packing the precious photos reminding her of happier times with her two guys.

After the moving van picked up the last of Laura's belongings, Terry and her husband drove Laura to the airport. Saying their goodbyes, the women hugged each other like children cling to their favorite teddy bear. They made a pact to keep in touch. Aboard the plane, Laura cried silent tears with her head propped back on the headrest and her eyes closed tightly. *I miss Mark and Derek so much. Why did this have to happen?* Although she'd never be the same, Laura decided to do something special with her life, in honor of her guys.

Chapter Seven

Marvice's Recurrent Dreams

As the months passed, Rich Marvice adjusted to his job as a postal carrier. Most of the time, his life brought him joy because Aggie and Jack motivated him to make each day happy. Since his talk with Aggie about the lost letters, Rich stopped having terrible nightmares. However, a strange, recurrent dream perplexed him. He spoke with his wife that night at supper. "Aggie," Rich said. He cleared his throat before continuing. "I've been having a strange dream—not a bad nightmare—but not a pleasant dream either. And I keep dreaming it over and over again. Sometimes, I wake up perspired, and I find myself holding my chest, even though I don't have any pain. It's weird."

"Rich, didn't you have a stress test for your physical before you started your new job?"

"Yes. The doctor said my heart's healthy."

"Oh . . . that's right." Aggie let out a deep breath. "Tell me about the dream."

"I'm running and running, away from someone or something. But the more I run, the heavier my legs feel, like I'm carrying weights on them."

"In your dream, where are you?"

"It's nighttime, before dark. I pass a mall, a school, and then a jail. That's when I wake up, holding my chest."

"Honey, I think it would be a good idea for you to see a therapist. Would you be willing? Now that you're working, we have great insurance. There's no need to worry about the money."

"I don't know, Aggie. I don't think I'd feel comfortable talking to a stranger about personal stuff."

"You could try. What do you have to lose? Maybe a therapist could help you get to the bottom of what's causing these strange dreams. Maybe it's related to the nightmares you were having when you first lost the letters."

"Maybe, but I put that behind me."

"It sure doesn't sound like you did, Rich!"

Chapter Eight

Jonathan Wright's Attempt

"I'll be right back," Jonathan Wright yelled to his wife Anne.

"Where are you off to in such a rush, Jon?" Anne asked.

"To mail this gift to David," he said. He gave her a peck on the cheek and whisked past her toward the door.

"Do you want me to mail it later when I go out?" she offered. "If I have time, I might go to the post office because I could use more stamps."

"Na. Thanks anyway. I need to bring a registration form to the civic center, so I'll put the card in the mailbox in front of the building." Jonathan closed the Victorian-style, red oak door and headed down the street toward the center of town.

When he reached the civic center and opened the mail chute, he realized he missed the last pickup at 11 a.m., but he decided to mail the card anyway. *Oh, well. The mail carrier would empty the box early Monday morning—not much different than if Anne had mailed the card at the post office later.* Jonathan went inside, turned in the registration form for his volunteering application, and headed home. He decided to take the longer, scenic route because the beautiful, brisk yet sunny Saturday tempted him to enjoy the outdoors. *Nice weather! I should call the guys about changing our golf night from Monday to Sunday. The weatherman said it looks like rain and heavy winds for Monday.*

A few blocks before he approached his house, Jonathan passed a young couple with a navy stroller. They smiled at each other and commented on their child's progress with his new bright, yellow-and-blue rubber toy attached to the front of the stroller. As the infant pushed the knobs on the toy in and out, his parents watched with glowing pride, discussing their son's remarkable hand and eye coordination. Seeing this family brought Jonathan back to the days when he and his ex-wife Melinda marveled over each and every accomplishment in David's life—no matter how minute. A part of him missed those days, even though his new life with Anne and the girls made him happy. The birth of one's first child is incredibly special, and he had been happy with Mel—for a while.

Jonathan wished things had been different with Melinda. He remembered when they met at college. She sat across from him in Art History. When she glanced his way, her blue-green, sparkling eyes immediately locked with his as if they had been lovers in another lifetime. They got married soon after graduating from college.

Although only twenty-three years old at the time she gave birth to David, Melinda managed to work about twenty to twenty-five hours a week as a freelance artist, traveling to the advertising agency to deliver her artwork, with David as her sidekick. Pleased with her work, Melinda's supervisor continued to employ her on a part-time basis until she could return full-time. Melinda seemed content sharing her life with Jonathan and David. But things started to change when her parents became ill.

Melinda wore too many hats, switching back and forth between them throughout the day, pulled in different directions. Her parents' illnesses brought challenges each day. Well-care visits for David overlapped with her mom's cancer treatments and her father's dialysis treatments. She tossed and turned at night, thinking about how to fit everything in that she needed to do the next day. Meanwhile, Jonathan worked long hours at the law firm, trying to climb his way up the corporate ladder. Their situation left little time for them to spend together.

Unfortunately, Jonathan often blamed Melinda for the distance in their relationship. He resented her role as the sole caregiver for her parents, which took time away from him. Melinda's brother, Eric, made excuses for why he couldn't take their parents for medical appointments, but he had time for poker tournaments. Jonathan and Melinda argued continually about confronting Eric. Jonathan would yell, "Why don't you ask your brother to help you?" Melinda would shout, "I'm their only daughter." She felt obligated to take care of her parents. They were good people who worked hard over the years to give their two children the best of everything. Although overwhelmed as a caregiver, Melinda loved her parents and took on the responsibility. In fact, she resented her husband's interference. She hated conflict and didn't want to alienate her only sibling.

Ironically, while she played the role of the docile sister, her home environment resembled a war zone. With Melinda stretched to the max juggling all of the appointments, working at home, and raising David, and Jonathan dealing with long hours at the law firm, the couple constantly fought, criticizing each other instead of working as a team. Eventually, the arguing between Jonathan and Melinda took a toll on their sex life. Looking for attention, Jonathan became involved with a young paralegal assistant, Anne, which ultimately led to divorcing Melinda when David was only four years old.

Approaching the lawn of his suburban colonial, Jonathan thought about the mistakes he made in his first marriage and sighed. *I fell in love with Melinda because of her strong compassion for others. How did I let my frustrations get in the way of her responsibilities and love for her parents? It wasn't fair to Mel. Why did*

I blame her when I fell out of love? Things worked out for me, though. I have a good life with Anne and our two daughters.

But Jonathan regretted the fact that he didn't spend enough time with his only son over the years. As he progressed in his law career, his life revolved around his job and related social functions. With Anne working as a paralegal assistant in the same firm, Jonathan didn't mind the crazy hours he spent there. However, his commitments left little time to be part of his son's life. Well before the birth of his two daughters, Jonathan became less and less involved in David's life. David grew up resenting his father for the numerous ball games and school plays he missed. Later, when David's half-siblings were born, he only heard from his father on special occasions, like his birthday and holidays. By the time David was seventeen, he became accustomed to not hearing much from his father, and he in turn contacted Jonathan less frequently.

Sadly, Jonathan remembered one of the last conversations he had with his son, before David's high school graduation. Jonathan had dropped the phone as he attempted to answer it while shuffling through paperwork on his desk. "Hi. Hold on one minute please." He looked at the number. "Oh. Hello Dave."

"Hi Dad. How are you?" his son asked, in an upbeat voice.

"Okay, son. I'm fine. Very busy with work though," Jonathan responded.

"How are the girls?"

"They're doing great. Growing taller by the minute," he chuckled.

"Dad, do you think you might be able to make it to my graduation this week? Mom said she mailed you a save-the-date note last month."

"I know, son. I wish I had the time, but I'm working on a really important case. I'm sorry."

"Oh, come on, Dad. You don't even have to stay for the whole thing." David's voice cracked like the dry sparks of a dwindling fire. "Just show up—for once—even at the end, for a picture with me."

"I'll try. It's just that it's crazy busy right now."

"Gee. Thanks," David replied, sarcastically. "Bye."

As Jonathan walked down the street toward his house, he recalled the night of David's graduation, when he went for drinks with a few of the lawyers and forgot about the ceremony. *I hope Dave will forgive me. The generous check I mailed to him as a graduation gift and my note promising to make more time for him should help.* Deep in thought, Jonathan tripped over a small tennis ball his daughters left on the front lawn. His foot slipped out of his moccasin and slid along the weeds of overgrown grass. *Jesus, the landscaper's late again.*

Anne opened the front door to let her husband inside. She kissed him on the cheek. "Jon. Are you okay?"

"Yeah, honey."

"Did you remember to hand in the volunteer registration form?"

"Yeah. I did," he said with disgust. "But I don't know how I'm going to make the time to help coach the girls' soccer team. I can barely make it to their games."

"Jon. It's important to the girls that you get more involved in their activities."

"I know, Anne, but you of all people should understand what my workload entails," he responded, irritated.

"Well, do your best when the time comes."

*   *   *

A few weeks passed when Jonathan realized he hadn't heard from David. Not a call. Not a thank-you note. It seemed strange because David always called to thank his father for gifts he sent. When Jonathan received his bank statement, he noticed that the check for David hadn't been cashed. *Could Dave be that* angry with me for missing his graduation that he didn't accept my gift?

Jonathan went to bed that night thinking about the relationships in his life. *Over the last few years, I managed to find time to spend with the girls—far more time than I ever spent with David. How did I let myself become such a neglectful father to him? I hope I haven't lost my chance to reconnect with him. Why hasn't David responded to my letter when I clearly apologized for missing the graduation and not spending enough time with him? Wouldn't he be happy to know that I finally came to my senses?* Eventually, Jonathan fell asleep, but he awoke several times, keeping Anne up, pulling at the sheets, huffing and puffing.

What's wrong, Jon?" Anne whispered, half-awake, half-asleep.

"I think I ruined my relationship with David. He finally had enough of my excuses," he whispered.

"Why don't you try calling him? Before you know it, he'll be leaving for Drexel. You still have time since David doesn't start until mid-September because of the trimesters. Don't you want to fix this before he leaves for college?"

"Yes, of course. He never ignored me like this," Jonathan said.

"I guess it didn't help that you wrote off his graduation night. Jon, I reminded you that morning. Remember?"

"Yeah. I know. I got caught up."

"Listen, Jon. Go to sleep. Call him tomorrow, and make plans to take him to dinner. Find out what he's thinking."

"What if . . ."

"If he doesn't answer his cell phone, call his mother. I'm sure she'll help you."

"I guess you're right," Jonathan said. He leaned over and hugged his wife. "Thanks, Annie. I love you."

"Me too. Now go to sleep."

* * *

The next morning before leaving for work, Jonathan tried reaching David on his cell phone. As he suspected, it went into voicemail. *I better call his mother.*

"Hello," said Melinda.

"Hi. Mel. It's Jonathan."

"Jonathan who? I think you have the wrong number," she said angrily. Melinda still felt extremely annoyed with her ex-husband for missing their son's graduation.

"Come on, Mel. I know I did wrong. I want to talk with my son."

"Oh, so *now* you want to talk to him. Two months after he graduated with honors."

"Listen, Mel. I sent him a check as a graduation gift."

"Isn't that just like you? Give some money, and it will make things all better."

"Mel, I sent him a card with a note too. I told him that I want to spend more time with him." Melinda didn't respond. "Mel, are you there?" Melinda took a deep breath. "Mel. Do you plan on answering me?"

Melinda finally gathered her thoughts. "David never mentioned a check—or a card."

"I'm sorry that I mailed it late, a few months after his graduation, because I was working crazy hours."

"Well, he's in the shower. I'll see what I can find out."

"Thanks, Mel. I appreciate it. I want to make this up to him. Tell him I'll pick him up at 7:00 tomorrow night. I'll be there—unless I hear otherwise from you or David."

"Okay, Jon. Bye." After Melinda hung up the phone, she sat back in her armchair. She closed her eyes, lost somewhere between amazed and confused. *Why did it take Jon over a decade to realize he's been an absentee father? I hope he truly means what he says.*

When Melinda talked to David, he said he didn't receive a gift or a card from his father. That surprised her because she knew that Jonathan broke promises but didn't deliberately lie. The card and the check must somehow have gotten lost in the mail. Melinda convinced her son to go to dinner with his father the following evening.

Chapter Nine

Jonathan's Reconciliation

onathan Wright arrived at Mel's condo at 6:45, anxious to prove his sincerity to David. His early arrival took Mel by surprise. She remembered the numerous times she waited with David on their sofa for Jonathan to pick him up for a visit. After a half hour passed and a new Disney program began, her son would say, "Mom, do you think Daddy forgot about me?" Always the soul-mender, Mel would say, "Of course not, David. You know your dad's usually late." But Mel resented her ex-husband for keeping their son waiting and fretting. After not seeing David all week, the least Jonathan could do was show up on time for the few hours he spent with him.

Mel chalked up Jonathan's newfound punctuality to Anne's influence. *It wouldn't be the first time a husband changed his ways the second time around. Anne and her daughters probably don't have to deal with Jonathan's lack of consideration. Well, at least he wants to rekindle his relationship with David.*

At 7 o'clock on the dot, David came down from his room. "Hi. I'm ready to go," he said with indifference. Mel's soft blue-green eyes turned stone-like as she glanced at her son. *It's unlike him to be cold to his father.* David's attitude mirrored his fragile, frustrated frame of mind.

* * *

Jonathan took David to Ristorante Sorella, a new Italian restaurant that opened near Mel's condo. While waiting for their meals to be served, Jonathan broke the ice. "Son, I want to start by apologizing for not making it to your graduation. I did wrong. I got caught up having drinks with the guys from work and planned on stopping by toward the end of the ceremony. But we all had too much to drink. I had to take a cab home and went straight to bed. I picked up my car early the next morning. There's a lot of pressure on me right now because the firm's looking to make one of us a partner. I know this doesn't excuse my behavior, but I wanted to tell you what happened that night."

"Yeah," David said.

"Then, I felt so guilty that it took me time to reach out to you. Call me an immature coward, because that's what I've been. But, I swear to you, I sent you a generous check as a graduation gift, along with a note in a card explaining what happened that night and how I want to be a better father to you," Jonathan added.

"Well, I never got a card with a check, or any kind of note," he responded, with a bit of suspicion in his voice.

"I mailed it at the postal box in front of the civic center. The mail is usually reliable. I'm not sure what happened. When I examined my bank statement and saw that you didn't cash the check, I assumed you were too mad to accept my gift or my effort at mending our relationship. I couldn't sleep at night, thinking I lost my son's love."

"Dad. You don't make it easy. For years you put me on the back burner. I know you work long hours, believe me, but you make the time for your new family. They're my half-sisters and I barely know them. It's as though when you left me and mom, you erased us from your life."

"I'm truly sorry, David. I want to make it up to you."

"It took you long enough. Why now—now that I'm leaving for college soon?"

"I'm not sure why it took me so long to grow up—to face the changes and challenges in my life. Son, you're more like your mother. I don't picture you ever neglecting one of your children. I'm truly ashamed of how I let you and your mom down. Things were easier with Anne."

"So, you want me to forget all of the years I cried for my dad to be a presence in my life?"

"No, David. Just think about it for a little while, and let me know. But don't make too much time pass. We already missed out on memories we could've made, and I'm not getting any younger," he laughed. Jonathan's lips shifted to one side. He portrayed a guilty smirk, like a school boy reminiscing about the fun, wild times of his youth.

After dinner, David told his father about the numerous scholarship offers he received. He talked at length about his friends and a girl he liked. It felt good for David to be able to share his life with his father. As for Jonathan, he felt like the proud dad who wheeled his son in his stroller, marveling at all of the new things he learned to do.

When Jonathan dropped David off four hours later, he gave his son a hug—something he hadn't done in a while. Both of them fought to hold back tears. This time, David believed his father. He'd go to bed truly happy. As David exited the car, Jonathan said, "Son. Here's your gift. I certainly wasn't taking a chance mailing this one." They both laughed, masking the strong emotions that permeated each of their minds.

"Thanks, Dad," David responded. "I'll wait for you to contact me first, since I know you're so busy."

"I promise I will, son. I enjoyed spending time with you. I'm proud of the man you've become and the successful future I know you'll have."

David smiled ear to ear and walked up the sandy-colored cobblestone path leading to the front door. When he got inside, he saw Melinda sipping tea while reading a book in her armchair. She looked unusually calm under the circumstances. Maybe she sensed a change in her ex-husband, or maybe she relied on her faith.

"How did it go with your father?" she asked David.

"Really good, Mom. He acted different this time, not distracted like the few times I saw him over the last couple of years. Would you believe he didn't look at his cell phone one time, not even to check if Anne left a message?"

Melinda laughed because she remembered how Jonathan clung to his cell phone. *He'd give up a frosty mug of beer before he'd abandon his cell phone. Wow he's reformed.* "David, I've been praying for your father to be more like the man I married. I wouldn't have fallen in love with him if he'd been an insensitive person. You know me better than that. David, the nuns at St. Joseph's Academy said that God hears the prayers of all of his children. It took some time, but I never gave up. I prayed, and prayed, and prayed."

Chapter Ten

Marvice's Confession

"**A**g, I mean it. If I lose sleep one more night due to these damn dreams, I'm gonna go crazy," Rich screamed.

"Rich, please let me make an appointment with a therapist. You can't go on like this. It's very strange. You go months without a problem, and then out of the blue the dreams start up again. I'm no psychologist, but something's tormenting you."

"I know, Ag. I think it's the guilt over those letters I lost. I couldn't even enjoy being named Employee of the Month. When my supervisor took my picture and put it on the board with the other winners, I felt like such a phony. How did I screw up so badly on my first day?"

"Look, Rich. You're a good worker. You earned that title. You've got to stop beating yourself up."

"Do you think I want to be tormented by these dreams?"

"That's not the point. You need to see a therapist," Aggie insisted. "Come on, Rich, it's not fair to me or Jack. He's noticed your on-again, off-again depression."

"Why? Did he say something about it?" Rich asked, concerned.

"I didn't want to add to your problems, but yesterday he asked me why daddy seems so sad."

"Oh, boy. I'm sorry, Ag. I don't want to hurt you or our son."

"Then please, Rich. See a therapist. At least try it."

"I don't feel comfortable. Besides, I talk to you all the time."

"But Rich, I'm not a professional. And it's too much pressure for me to deal with your depression. We need to consider our child and the effects on him." Aggie looked into her husband's despondent, tear-soaked eyes—eyes that used to sparkle like glistening ice crystals in the moonlight. She hurt for her husband.

After a few minutes of silence, Rich perked up, as though an explosion of energy rushed through his veins, electrifying him deep in his soul, bringing brightness back into his eyes. He turned to his wife, kissed her forehead, and said, "Aggie. I'm going to do what I needed to do years ago."

Aggie wondered if her husband had lost it altogether. "What do you mean?" she asked.

"Ag. I'm going to my supervisor tomorrow morning and confessing the details of that day—the day I lost those three letters."

"Now! Oh my God, Rich. Are you sure about this?"

"Most definitely. It's the only way for me to get peace."

"Oh, boy. How do you think he'll react?"

"I don't know, but I have to talk to him. I pride myself on being honest. He's a family man, and I think he'll understand why I kept this from him."

"Okay, hon. But promise me that you'll see a therapist if the dreams continue."

"All right, Ag. I may need a therapist depending on my boss's reaction," he said, laughing through a half-worried smile.

* * *

Before entering his supervisor's office, Rich Marvice took a deep, deep breath. *Be a man. You gotta do this.* Rich knocked on the door and stepped into Bob Clayton's office. "Good morning, Bob," he said politely.

"Good morning," Bob responded. "How's the family?"

"Real good, thanks. Ag and I are enjoying Jack growing up. You know what it's like having kids. They become your whole world. How's your family?"

"Good too, thanks. What can I do for you?" Bob asked.

Rich took another deep breath and began his confession. "I need to talk to you about something that happened to me the first day on the job."

"Really?" He seemed surprised. "How many years ago?"

"Two."

"Hum. Two years goes fast, doesn't it?"

Rich didn't answer. If only Bob knew how slowly it went for him. "Bob. Let me start by saying how much I appreciate my job. It means the world to me. It allows me to take care of my family and have a sense of security." Bob listened attentively as he always did. Rich continued, "On my first day, two years ago, it rained like hell. I handled the rain, trying my best not to get the mail wet. The wind. Well, it shook everything in its path. At one point, I gathered up the mail at the box in front of the civic center in Caldwell. I had a batch in my hands and began to transfer it to my bag when a super-strong wind almost knocked me to my knees. A few of the letters—I think three of them—fell out of my hands. As I bent to pick them up, another gust of wind ripped them from my fingers, and I lost them down the sewer."

Finally, Rich felt free of the heavy weight that bound him like chains for two years. With each sentence Rich Marvice spoke, the secret burden he carried around left him. His conscience cleared as each guilt-laden, built-up feeling of anxiety peeled away a little at a time, like layers of an onion stripped to the core. He breathed a sigh of relief, as he waited for Bob's response.

Bob looked at Rich in disbelief. From the beginning, Rich had been one of his best workers—always on time, dedicated to his job, pleasant to everyone, and sincere. Bob took a sip from the coffee cup on his desk and then said, "Rich, I appreciate you coming to me about this. You're a good man. To be honest with you, I don't know if we would've been able to retrieve the letters from the sewer. Between the rain and the rubbish they were probably destroyed—if not chewed up by rats." Bob laughed and looked at Rich to see his reaction. "I understand that accidents happen. Some things we can't control. You might not have realized it your first day on the job, but you can come to me with any problem, and I will work through it with you. I even have a good ear if you need personal advice."

"Bob, I deeply appreciate your understanding. I haven't been at peace since the incident, worrying about what impact the loss of those letters might've had on people's lives."

"I wouldn't worry, Rich. If any of the letters were that important, in the end, the senders would find a way to make contact with their intended recipients. If any of them were bills, well, bills do get lost in the mail sometimes."

"You know, Bob. That's exactly what Aggie said to me, but I wish I had come to you from the start. I felt a lot of pressure and didn't want to risk being fired. I know that's not an excuse, and I'm sorry for my negligence and for not coming clean sooner."

"Don't lose any more sleep over this, Rich. Things have a way of working out, with or without our hands in them."

On his way out of the office, Rich shook Bob's hand and thanked him again. He felt fortunate to have such a considerate supervisor.

*   *   *

That night at supper, Rich Marvice fully enjoyed his time with his family. Aggie made his favorite meal—lasagna—knowing he might need some comfort food, or maybe a celebratory dinner. Elated, she saw the huge smile on her husband's face as he walked through the front door, whistling a nursery rhyme for Jack. Rich gently kissed them both, washed his hands at the sink, and sat at the dinner table. He told Aggie about his talk with Bob, but he didn't dwell on it. He didn't need to say much because his cheery demeanor spoke for him. Aggie hoped and prayed that Rich's confession would help him find peace and end his nightmares.

Over the next few months, Rich slept better than he had in the two years after the mail debacle. Although he continued to have nightmares once in a while, they were less disturbing. In time, they ended altogether. That's not to say that he forgot about the lost letters. Occasionally, he'd wonder about who sent them and why. When such thoughts crossed his mind, he hoped that all of the people involved were leading happy, successful lives like him. Rich Marvice, who felt like the luckiest man in the world, had a wife who stood by him through tough times, a doting son, and a job he enjoyed.

Chapter Eleven

Over the Next Ten Years

Miabella Maxima

During the first semester of her sophomore year, Miabella kept a low profile on campus because she didn't want to bump into Alex. Only a year ago, she felt elated to be his girlfriend, but everything fell apart that September due to a stupid misunderstanding. She tried explaining things to Alex when he called her, accusing her of cheating, but he refused to listen. Hoping to gain his trust, she poured her heart out in an apology letter. She did her best to explain that she didn't have romantic feelings for her friend Joe, but Alex never reached out to her. Miabella struggled with the fact that he rejected her and hooked up with another girl so quickly.

For the rest of the semester, she avoided him completely, both at school and at local hangouts. It's not that she didn't want to talk to him; she still loved him. He'd always hold a special place in her heart, but her pride wouldn't allow her to approach him. The few times Miabella saw Alex walking arm in arm with his bleached-blonde girlfriend, it made her stomach churn. With her head held high, she walked in the opposite direction, unnoticed by either of them.

But no matter how much Miabella avoided Alex, she couldn't stop thinking about him. The same questions kept haunting her. *Did he ever miss me? Was everything he told me a lie to get me to sleep with him?*

I thought I knew Alex better than that. Was I wrong? Miabella never imagined she'd be replaced so easily. She wanted to return to the carefree, trusting girl she used to be. With a broken compass and a heavy heart, it would take some time to find her way home.

*   *   *

Despite her intense feelings for Alex, Miabella decided that their broken relationship wouldn't define her. She'd push ahead and emerge stronger. For the time being, however, she had no desire to date. Whenever a guy on campus asked her out, she'd make up an excuse, trying not to offend him. Instead, she threw herself into her schoolwork, managing to keep up a 3.9 grade point average.

During the second semester of her sophomore year, Miabella made a bold decision: She transferred to Boston College. When she initially applied to colleges her senior year of high school, she got acceptance letters from a few prestigious, out-of-state universities, but she chose to attend WP so that she could live at home. Now, Mia needed a change. She'd miss her family and her large, comfortable, beautifully decorated bedroom. She'd miss her high school friends who were attending local colleges, although they promised to visit her in Boston. A year and a half ago, Miabella couldn't imagine leaving her comfort zone, but now she needed to move on, and Vicky understood that best. Vicky comforted Mia the many nights she cried over a pint of Eddy's slow-churned rocky road ice cream. Miabella didn't want to end her college experience avoiding Alex and his new girlfriend and missing out on life. Vicky understood the stress that Mia handled being on the same campus as them. After Miabella gave herself to Alex completely, he hurt her deeply.

* * *

During her senior year at Boston College, Miabella met her husband, Brandon Ewing. They were interning at the same pharmaceutical company and spent a lot of time in the lab alone, working on various projects. Their long hours together drew them closer and closer. Before Miabella could put up her defenses, she started having feelings for Brandon—feelings she hadn't experienced since Alex. One night, after a romantic, candle-lit dinner at a waterfront restaurant, Brandon swept Mia off her feet with a tender kiss at her front door before she could find an excuse to avoid being intimate with him. Over the next few months, a rush of magical feelings that melted away her wall took hold of Miabella until they led her down the church aisle to meet Brandon at the altar and, later, toward a house in the suburbs of Massachusetts.

Over the next five years, Miabella and Brandon had three children—two boys and a girl. Miabella's parents would drive to Massachusetts to visit them, but as the Maximas got older, travel became increasingly difficult.

Mia and Brandon decided to bring the children to see their grandparents in Caldwell whenever they could take time off from work.

One Saturday morning when Miabella and her family were visiting her parents in Caldwell, she decided to cook dinner. She planned a special meal to share with her parents—an antipasto appetizer, a pasta dish with shrimp and lobster, and her famous chocolate pudding pie. As Mia put on her jacket, she yelled out, "I'll be back soon." She glanced at her family. The Maximas were playing monopoly with the kids. Brandon looked up from his laptop, put his fingers to his lips, and blew her a kiss. Mia's smile expressed her love for her husband.

Driving to the Shop Rite, Miabella looked around at the surroundings she called home for many years. Although she stayed in touch with Vicky, she lost contact with most of her other high school friends. Vicky and Mia managed to meet once or twice a year in Connecticut, about halfway between their homes.

Miabella decided to call Vicky later and invite her friend to her parents' house for dessert. Vicky married a guy she met at WP, had a boy and a girl, and bought a house in Caldwell. It would be great for their children to spend time together.

Walking through the Shop Rite, Miabella noticed the setup was the same as when she left the area to move to Boston. She walked down the produce aisle to pick up vegetables she needed to cook for dinner. While holding a plump tomato in her hand, checking it for soft spots, she heard a familiar, sexy voice.

"Mia. Is that you?" asked a handsome, brown-haired, dark-eyed guy in jeans and a T-shirt.

Miabella turned around and looked into that pair of soft olive-like eyes she treasured as a young girl. "Alex?"

"You look great, Mia. Did you move back from Boston?" he asked, appearing a little nervous and uncomfortable.

"No. I'm visiting my parents. They're getting too old to make the trip to my house, so we decided to visit them for the holidays," Mia replied, realizing that *we* indicated a special someone in her life. She wondered if Alex ever got married. Once Mia left for Boston, she decided to not look back. She didn't want Vicky to tell her anything she might know about Alex's life.

"Oh. How long will you be here?"

"Five days. My husband and I have to get back to our jobs." *There, I said it. I broke the ice.*

"Mia, would you have time to go to the café with me—just for a half hour?"

Mia hesitated for a minute and then said, "Sure. I just got here. My carriage is empty. I'll come back later."

As Miabella and Alex walked across the street to the café, she felt confident about what she planned to say. She'd finally have a face-to-face talk with Alex about her unanswered letter and the incidents that led her to fill her stationary with tears and emotion. At the café,

Mia ordered a cup of hazelnut coffee, and Alex did the same. She remembered they both loved hazelnut. *Some things never change.* Mia decided to ask the question that needed to be asked. "Alex, did you ever get married?"

"Yeah, Mia."

"To?"

"To Tamara, the blonde girl I met at WP."

"Oh," breathed Miabella. "Do you have any children?"

"No. Tamara doesn't want any. She doesn't have much patience for children." He laughed.

"But I thought you wanted kids," said Mia, almost sympathetically.

"Yeah. I did. But it didn't work out that way," he replied. Mia could see the look of regret in Alex's big brown eyes. She felt sorry for him. Her children brought her much joy.

After the waitress served the coffee, Mia decided to bring up the letter. She took a hearty sip for encouragement. "Alex," she said softly, trying not to sound as though she was attacking him, "why did you totally ignore the letter I sent you after we broke up?"

Alex gulped down some coffee, placed his cup in front of him, and looked at Miabella, puzzled. "What letter?" he asked.

"Come on, Alex. It's ten years later. If I can talk about it, you should be able to. We've both gone on with our lives."

"Mia, I don't know what letter you're talking about."

"Alex, I mailed a letter apologizing for the misunderstanding about the kiss. I told you how much I cared about you and how I wanted to work things out. And I left the ball in your court, only you never called me."

"Mia, I swear. I'm telling the truth. I never got the letter. The reason I wanted to have coffee with you is to apologize for acting like such a jerk. I should have spoken to you in person instead of saying everything in a phone call. I couldn't accept that someone else made you happier. Kara cheated on me, but I never expected you to be with someone else after . . ."

"After I slept with you? You can say it Alex. I'm all grown up now. I have three kids," Miabella said.

Alex saw a different Miabella than he knew. Still beautiful years later, she glowed with a captivating confidence that made her even more unattainable. Her maturity showed as she talked about their past, uninhibited. "Mia, I'm sorry, but I never got a letter from you."

"I guess it disappeared somewhere. Does your family lose mail?" she asked, half laughing, half in disbelief.

"Not really."

"Well, will you listen to me now, so you'll understand the situation better and have some resolution?"

"Sure," said Alex, "but I have one more apology. I'm sorry I started seeing Tamara right away. It wasn't fair to you. I owed it to you to talk things over."

"Thanks, Alex. I guess we both grew up a bit." Mia smiled. "I've know Joe, the boy who John saw me kissing, since we were kids. I love him like a brother, but I never had romantic feelings for him. Joe said his feelings for me changed when I got closer to you."

Alex interrupted, "You mean you told him about, you know?"

"No. Not at all. I wouldn't tell Joe that we made love. I guess he developed romantic feelings for me over time, but I didn't feel the same way. When he kissed me, it caught me off-guard. I didn't know how to react, until he leaned in to kiss me again, and I stopped him. Joe's a great guy, Alex. He never pressured me after that. He even asked if he could do anything to help us get back together, but I told him it was all up to you."

"Gee. Mia. I don't know what to say."

"Well, it doesn't matter now. We can't change the past," she said. *I wonder if my letter would have made a difference back then anyway.*

"I'm glad you're happy, Mia. I bet you're a great mom," Alex said. Mia saw that look of regret on Alex's face again.

"I am—at least that's what they tell me." Miabella laughed. She finally got to speak her truth. She believed Alex when he said he never received her letter. The sincerity showed in his big brown eyes.

Alex picked up the tab for the coffee, like old times. After Miabella thanked him, she stood up and put her arm into the sleeve of her jacket, getting ready to go back to the grocery store. "I'd better hurry up," she said. "My family will wonder if I've gone to Italy to pick up the stuff for the antipasto."

Alex helped Miabella put her other arm into her jacket and stared into her eyes when she turned around. "You look great, Mia." He hesitated for a minute and said, "Can I hug you goodbye?"

With wide-open, tear-filled eyes, Miabella stepped toward Alex and gave him a huge hug. "It was good to see you Alex. I hope you have a happy life."

"You too, Mia," he said, in almost a whisper. Alex watched Miabella walk away. *How could I have been so stupid? Well, life seemed to work out okay for both of us.*

* * *

Miabella walked back to the Shop Rite and quickly finished food shopping. While rushing down the aisles, she thought about her conversation with Alex. Memories of their past relationship flipped through her mind, quickly turning from image to image, resembling faded pictures in an old, dusty photo album of loved ones long gone. Miabella felt choked up with emotion when she hugged Alex goodbye, but the magic that raced through her body whenever he touched her seemed as distant as the memories that forced their way into her thoughts. *I have to tell Brandon about seeing Alex, but I'll wait 'till after dinner.*

Throughout the night, however, Brandon sensed Miabella's preoccupation. Alone with Miabella in her old bedroom, Brandon spoke before she could tell him about bumping into Alex. "Mia. You seemed distracted tonight. What's on your mind?" he asked, placing his comforting arm around her petite shoulders. Mia looked into her husband's loving eyes. They had a relationship that she believed could survive any problem. Miabella trusted Brandon completely, and he never doubted her fidelity, devotion, and love. She didn't fear talking to him about sensitive issues. True, she loved Alex in the past. But when she fell in love with Brandon, she realized that her relationship with Alex lacked one important quality—trust. That lack of trust tore them apart.

Miabella placed her head on Brandon's shoulder and said, "I saw Alex at the Shop Rite. We went to the café and talked for a while. He never got my letter, but it doesn't matter to me now."

Brandon hugged Miabella in a strong yet tender embrace. He looked at her and said exactly what she needed to hear, "That must have been hard for you, Mia. Do you feel better now?" Mia smiled and nodded yes. Her decision to change colleges helped her get away from Alex and Tamara, but destiny brought her to Brandon. Mia treasured Brandon and their children. She wouldn't trade them for anyone—not even Alex. That night, Mia made love to her husband with an intense passion, savoring each kiss as it aroused her body and heart. A part of her would always care about Alex, but she found her soul mate in Brandon. Her desire for Brandon grew profoundly with each passing year.

* * *

Laura Spelling

When she first moved to Las Vegas, Laura felt defeated each day. Her sister Sarah talked her into seeing a therapist to help her deal with her conflicting emotions and terrible losses. At times, when Laura tried to relax watching TV, she wondered if she should have persistently pursued a meeting with the boy who shot her son so she could get closure. Other times, she thought it best that she never see his face or expressions. *Why in the world did I think I could handle seeing this boy? Would I break down and cry before I opened my mouth to speak?* In therapy, Laura dealt with these feelings and talked about ways to move forward and feel fulfilled without Mark and Derek by her side.

One night while attending a charity event for disadvantaged youth, Laura made a decision that set her on a path toward a new life. She listened to a mother's touching story about her autistic son. The mother recalled a family birthday party that turned into a nightmare for him. The talking, laughing, and pounding feet of children as they ran back and forth tremendously disturbed the boy. He cupped his hands over his ears, trying to block out the noise. Then he ran toward the nearest door and motioned that he wanted to leave. His father gently lifted him up, hugged him, waved goodbye to his wife, and left the party to take the boy home. The mother's eyes filled with tears as she explained the feeling of watching all of the other children playing happily and eating birthday cake.

Another mother at the event, whose son had a severe case of Down syndrome, spoke about how much time it took for him to complete a small task. One of the projects at the therapy center he attended involved placing screws of different lengths in plastic containers, which had separate compartments for the different sizes of screws. On a good day, the boy placed all of the larger screws in the appropriate compartment with the therapist's help within an hour. On a bad day, he barely got through placing half of the screws.

Hearing these stories, Laura thought about Derek. Although he hadn't dealt with the challenges these kids faced, his life ended before he could show the world his talents. Laura brushed these feelings away, covering them until her mind emptied like a blank canvas. Then, something wonderful happened. Her canvas filled with a glowing picture of a young boy who needed her help grasping a paintbrush to create his masterpiece. The boy smiled at her with a genuine look of gratitude. Laura blinked her eyes, refocused on the presenters, and listened to one incredible story after another. By the end of the evening, she decided to go back to college to train as a special education teacher.

After completing her education, Laura Spelling found fulfillment teaching at a school for special needs children. Each day she entered her classroom, she felt the presence of Derek and Mark. *How happy they would be to know I did something useful with my life, giving back to the world, despite my losses!* Yet, working as a special education teacher proved challenging. At the end of the day, Laura relaxed with a soothing bubble bath, a cup of hot green tea, and a mystery novel or a crossword puzzle.

A year passed, and Laura settled in her new life in Las Vegas. She purchased a townhouse close to Sarah's home, and she often visited her sister and her family. Laura made new friends among the faculty members. On Friday nights, the women went to dinner. At some point in the evening, the subject of match-matching surfaced. Laura's new friends were married, and they wished she had a significant other to take to dinner with the couples on Saturday nights.

But Laura needed time to heal, not a boyfriend. She had trouble falling asleep without Mark at her side. Sometimes, she'd dream about Mark and Derek. In a recurring dream, her two guys played basketball in the driveway. They laughed heartily, trying to outdo each other to win whatever bet they made. Laura felt that familiar happiness of watching her husband and son grow closer. Then, the dream took an ominous turn. The ball whirled around the rim like a crazed, unrecognizable object, bounced off with a loud thump, and disappeared into blackness. Laura would awaken, sit up in bed, and stare at the walls, crying.

*   *   *

One morning, the faculty received an announcement that the principal planned to retire early due to health reasons. To take his place, the superintendent hired a male principal with previous experience. The hallways buzzed with conversations about the new, good-looking administrator, Alan O'Shanley. Alan, a forty-nine-year-old widower, had two children—a twelve-year-old boy and a nine-year-old girl. His wife died in a car crash several years prior, and he never remarried.

A few days before his arrival, Alan scheduled a luncheon with his staff. At noontime, one by one the teachers and aides filed into the lunch room to meet their new administrator. Some of the teachers introduced themselves before the meeting began; they agreed that the principal seemed kind and easy-going. Alan began speaking to the group before Laura arrived. She couldn't go to the luncheon on time because one of her students refused to leave with his mother for a doctor appointment. Within ten minutes, she managed to calm the child, and they left.

Laura rushed down the hall, worried about the impression she'd make with the new administrator. When she opened the door in a hurry, it flung open. "Sorry I'm late," she said. Laura felt embarrassed and hoped no one could see her pounding heart as she struggled to catch her breath.

"That's fine. Please sit down and join the rest of the faculty," Alan said. Alan continued his brief presentation. When he finished, everyone enjoyed a variety of sub sandwiches and salads. While the deli workers served the coffee and dessert, Alan walked around the room, attempting to speak to his staff in one-on-one conversations. Most of the teachers asked him about his previous position and what brought him to their school. He felt an instant connection to Laura, who spoke on a more personal level than most of the teachers.

"I heard you have children. How old are they?" she asked, already knowing the answer thanks to hallway gossip.

"My son Michael is twelve, and my daughter Ashleigh is nine," he answered. The gleam in his eyes showed pride.

"They must keep you busy, but a nice kind of busy, right?" she asked.

"You sound like you speak from experience. Do you have any children?"

Laura hesitated for a minute and gathered her strength. She didn't want to cry during her first encounter with the new administrator. She spoke softly but with a sense of acceptance. "I had a son, but he passed away a few years ago."

"Oh, I'm so sorry to hear that," Alan said. His jovial tone changed.

"Thank you, but I'm doing much better." Laura decided to change the subject. "Are you enjoying your first day so far?" she asked.

"Everything is going quite well, thank you. I'm trying to talk to as many teachers as possible, but I'm sure I'll confuse everyone's names." His beautiful smile caught Laura's attention. From the corner of his eyes, Alan could see that his secretary needed him. "Excuse me," he blurted, "but I think I'm being summoned. Nice to meet you, Ms. . . .?"

"Spelling. My name's Laura Spelling. Nice to meet you too."

Alan joined his secretary to answer questions about a busing problem. He said his goodbyes to his staff and then walked toward his office. On the way down the hall, he kept thinking about Laura Spelling. *What a sincere, attractive woman. Hmm. I didn't see a wedding ring.*

Walking back to her classroom for the afternoon session, Laura daydreamed about Alan. She hadn't paid much attention to the rumors about his good looks, although they turned out to be true. His full, dark-brown hair, styled neatly, made him look years younger. *What stunning blue eyes! He's so handsome and compassionate.* But Laura felt something beyond a physical attraction. In their short conversation, Alan's expressions and concern for her revealed a man of character.

* * *

Over the next few months, Alan and Laura became good friends. She met his children and cooked several meals for the family. She could tell Michael and Ashleigh missed their mother by the way they spoke about her. One night, Laura made a pot roast with potatoes and carrots. After Ashleigh's first bite, she looked at Laura and said, "Wow. It tastes like Mom's."

Laura didn't mind being compared to Alan's widow. After all, she helped raise wonderful children.

When Laura returned home, she'd remember times with Mark and Derek. She still struggled with loneliness and anxiety. While watching TV, her mind wandered. *How would Mark and Derek feel about my new life? I think they'd be proud of me for being so strong. Mark always encouraged me to go back to college. He'd be happy that I'm a full-fledged teacher.*

Although Laura would never be able to replace Mark and Derek, Alan and his children became increasingly important to her. They understood the sadness she felt because they also experienced tragedy. Their mutual losses and need to rebuild their lives was the link that joined them together. Three years after they met, Alan asked Laura to marry him, and she accepted. Neither one ever imagined they'd find love again, but they did.

* * *

Laura Spelling O'Shanley found enjoyment and a sense of purpose through teaching, and security and love with a kind man. When she married Alan, she took on the role of stepmother to two fantastic children—a role she treasured. However, at times, she thought about the boy who killed her son. *What a terrible situation for Louis and his family!*

One day, Laura called Terry, asking her to find out whatever she could about Louis. Terry's husband spoke to several people in the judicial system until he learned a little about the boy's situation. In prison, Louis Chalez acted like a model citizen. But, due to the fact that armed robbery of a bank is considered a federal crime, he couldn't get out early for good behavior. Yet, he made the best of his situation, completing his GED and earning a college degree online.

Louis spent many sleepless nights reliving the events of that awful day. He kept a journal as a form of therapy. The pages of his journal held his heartfelt thoughts—his deep regret for taking the life of an innocent bystander about the same age as him. Most of all, Louis worried about his mother and his family, and he felt sorrow for causing Derek's mom unbearable pain. According to Terry's source, Louis wrote a book about the mess he made of his life, hoping to stop other poor, struggling kids from making a similar mistake. He dedicated his book to his mom, to Mrs. Spelling, and to all the moms who lost children in fatal shootings.

Ultimately, Louis' mother managed to raise her other children without her son's help despite her desperate circumstances. Putting her pride aside, she filled out paperwork for government assistance. She joined a support group, where she met women who offered to babysit for her children. Eventually, Mrs. Chalez returned to work full-time and no longer relied on assistance. Each day, however, she worried about Louis and longed for his freedom, which wouldn't happen until after his thirty-sixth birthday. Despite her misgivings about prison life, Mrs. Chalez felt proud that her son continued his education and had the courage to write a book about his mistakes so he could help others. She hoped, after his release from prison, Louis would live his adult life in a peaceful and happy existence.

*   *   *

Jonathan Wright

God answered Melinda Wright's prayers; after years of being an absentee father, her ex-husband stepped up to the plate and mended the relationship with their son. When Jonathan's note and graduation gift for David got lost in the mail, it forced him to take action. Faced with the possibility of alienating his only son after blowing off his graduation, Jonathan reflected on his behavior and took steps to gain David's love and trust. He also appreciated Melinda's role as a mother. If she hadn't encouraged David to give his dad another chance, they probably would have grown further apart.

Before David left for Drexel, Jonathan reached out to Melinda with a phone call.

"Hello," Melinda answered. Her anxious tone revealed the pressure she put on herself to make sure she packed everything David needed for his first semester away from home.

"Hi, Mel. It's Jonathan."

"Oh. Hi, Jon. What can I help you with? I'm in the middle of doing things," she replied.

"Well, um. Could I accompany you and David when he leaves for Drexel? I wouldn't stay the entire weekend, but I thought our son would appreciate my support."

"It's okay with me, and I'm sure it will make David happy." *Wow, what a change.* "What about Anne?"

"I'll take care of it," he replied. "I also want to apologize for not being a strong presence in our son's life after the divorce. I should have made time for David, but I didn't. I'll make it up to both of you."

"I'm glad to hear that. All I need is for you to be there for David as much as possible. That's all I need to make me happy," Melinda said.

*   *   *

Whenever David returned from Drexel for a visit, Jonathan invited him to dinner at his home with Anne and their two daughters, Alyssa and Rebecca. Once the girls spent time with David, they were thrilled to have their older brother in their lives. He played softball with them, listened to their endless stories, and even dressed like a court jester for their royal-themed puppet show.

Alyssa and Rebecca filled a void in David's life. Although Melinda had always tried to keep her son busy with activities and play dates, he felt lonely growing up as an only child. When David visited his friend Greg's house, and watched him horsing around with his brother, he wished he had a brother or sister to tease. Now, David felt special having younger sisters who looked up to him.

In time, Anne got over her jealous feelings when she realized the positive influence David had on her daughters and her husband. Jonathan appeared more relaxed since he mended his relationship with his son. Once Anne got to know David, she really liked him. One night, she felt compelled to praise Mel for the job she did raising David. "You know, Jon," she said, as she picked up a cotton ball, soaked it in makeup remover, and applied it to her eyes. "Dave's a great kid. I know I've been a bit jealous of your ex—after all, she gave you a son—but I have to say that she did a great job as a parent."

"I'm glad to hear you say that because I've felt conflicted for years. I never wanted you to think that you and the girls weren't my priority, but Dave's my flesh and blood too." Anne turned away from the mirror, toward her husband, to listen. "Come over here by me," he said, pointing to the edge of their bed, where he reclined with a newspaper. Jonathan reached for Anne's arm and pulled her in for a quick kiss. As he looked into her eyes, he said, "It feels great to know you understand."

Anne smiled at her husband. "Jon, I'm sorry if I made things difficult for you, but you proved it's never too late to make a tough situation better."

"True. I'm amazed how it took one lost piece of mail to put the fear of God in me. Not hearing from my son at that time made me come to my senses. I wish I could thank the person who lost my darn mail!"

End

Acknowledgments

Thanks to Wendy Decker and Pat Florio for all of the awesome suggestions that helped me bring my characters to life. I am grateful for everything I learned.

Thanks to Mary Louise for inspiring me to write my first full-length work. I'll always remember her effervescent smile and encouraging words, "In life, you have to take chances."

Thanks to my husband Ron for all his support. Also, special thanks to my son Ron, Jr., who listened to my ideas and helped me develop the story lines.

Bío

Tina Marie Sausa grew up in northern New Jersey. Over the years, she has worked as an English teacher and as an editor in various technical fields. She lives with her husband and son.